D1711382

TRAIL OF THE BEAR

Center Point
Large Print

Also by D. B. Newton and available from
Center Point Large Print:

Bounty on Bannister
Bullets on the Wind
Syndicate Gun
Broken Spur
Fury at Three Forks
Range Boss

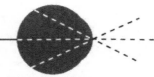

TRAIL OF THE BEAR

D. B. Newton

CENTER POINT LARGE PRINT
THORNDIKE, MAINE

This Center Point Large Print edition
is published in the year 2023 by arrangement with
Golden West Inc.

First US edition: Popular Library.

The text of this Large Print edition is unabridged.
In other aspects, this book may vary
from the original edition.
Printed in the United States of America
on permanent paper sourced using
environmentally responsible foresting methods.
Set in 16-point Times New Roman type.

ISBN 978-1-63808-937-7 (hardcover)
ISBN 978-1-63808-941-4 (paperback)

The Library of Congress has cataloged this record
under Library of Congress Control Number: 2023942209

CHAPTER I

The three men in sweat-stained cavalry uniforms—two troopers and a sergeant, all of them big, all of them tough specimens with faces browned by field duty and Montana weather—seemed to be enjoying themselves baiting the old Indian. They had him ringed, afoot amid their horses, standing there in the sun in his castoff white man's clothing, with a limp gunny sack slung over one shoulder. He had his shoulders hunched and was trying without much success to keep an eye on all three as he silently glared at his tormentors.

They wanted the gunny sack, and he was just as fiercely determined not to let them have it. Now one of the troopers, seeing his attention was occupied, kneed his horse a cautious step toward his blind side and bent to reach from the saddle, but sharp ears caught the sound and the old man quickly wheeled aside. The movement carried him too near the sergeant, however; the latter saw his chance and, leaning, deftly snatched the gunny sack away from him. When the Indian whirled, clawing for it like a wildcat, the non-com simply put a boot in his narrow chest and sent him into the dirt, hard.

5

"Now, Chief," he said, showing his strong white teeth in a grin—he had a thick sandy mustache and cruel eyes. "We have to check and see what you got from your friend in the tradin' post." He pointed with his chin to the low log building at the edge of the timber, a hundred yards away; smoke lifted from a stone chimney built against the near end of it, but otherwise there was no movement, no indication anyone had noticed or was paying attention to what was happening here. "If there's whiskey, you know we have to confiscate it. You know the law don't allow sellin' likker to no Injun."

Not trying to rise, the old man glared balefully through a tangle of graying hair. "No whiskey," he retorted. But the sergeant, taking the sack by a bottom corner, upended it.

He shook the sack and its contents spilled out—a half dozen potatoes, an onion, a small bag of salt, three air-tights. Nothing else. The sergeant looked scornfully at the items scattered on the ground, and lifted a thick shoulder. "Well, all I can say, it's a good thing we *didn't* find no bottle. You could of been in real trouble. You know that, don't you, Chief? Don't you?" he repeated, prodding, but the Indian's mouth was set like a trap. The sergeant's grin only widened, without touching his eyes.

One of the troopers laughed outright. "Looks like you're gonna have to buy your own, Bailey."

"Hell!" the non-com retorted. "What are you talking about? No self-respecting white man would insult his stomach with the rotgut they pass off on these savages!" He looked again at the Indian, his eyes speculative—as though he wasn't yet through with the old man, and debated what further sport he could have here. "Well?" he said heavily, indicating the contents of the sack littering the ground at his horse's feet. "You gonna pick all this stuff up? You red scum live like pigs—got no pride at all, scattering your trash like that."

He got no answer. The Indian, unmoving, peered up at him like a cornered animal. Saddle leather creaked as one of the troopers shifted position, as though boring of the game. Wind made a sound like surf through the pines at fire timber's edge, and brought a tang of smoke carried from the trading post's chimney.

Sergeant Bailey still held the gunny sack. He dangled it invitingly and said, "If you want this junk, come pick it up." But the hatred in the unwinking stare of the Indian was tempered now with caution—clearly, he was wary of letting himself get within the white man's reach. And suddenly the sergeant lost his temper. "You gonna do what you're told?" He flung down the sack as one hand moved threateningly toward the service revolver in his holster.

That was the moment when a new voice said,

at the sergeant's back, "Don't you think this has gone about far enough?"

The troopers had been so engrossed in what they were doing that they had missed the approach of another horseman, following the wagon road out of the trees. Startled, now, their heads jerked around and the non-com pivoted his horse in a tight half-circle; he glared at the man sitting saddle a dozen feet away—a slight but sturdy figure in a cowpuncher's denims, dark-featured, and with sharp black eyes that peered at him beneath the Stetson's brim. The young fellow's horse, a black, appeared to be a good one; the stock saddle and rig looked serviceable, and so did the holstered gun belted around his waist. The sergeant considered the gun for a moment, and the angry black eyes in the hawklike, coppery face. He said heavily, "Did you think you were talking to me?"

"I wouldn't know who else," the newcomer said, without any change of expression. "Looks plain enough you're the one that's been giving him the bad time. Why don't you let him alone?"

One of the troopers cut in on him. "Boy, you know you're dealing with the U. S. Cav'lry?"

But the sergeant was already speaking. "When I need advice how to deal with a mangy Injun, I ain't likely to ask another one! Now, Rain-in-the-Face, you'd best git on back to the reservation while I'm of a mind to overlook you butting into my affairs!" The non-com let a stare rest on the stranger for a moment, giving emphasis to his warning. Afterward he turned back to his victim. "I told *you* to get over here and start picking up this trash."

The old man had got to his knees, but he rose no farther. He shook his head stubbornly. And at that, Bailey really lost his temper. "By God, I'm tired bein' backtalked by lousy redskins!" His paw of a hand settled on his gun, started to pull it from the holster.

"Leave that where it is!" the stranger said, with a note in his voice that made the sergeant freeze with caution. Weapon half out of the leather, he whipped his head about and saw the revolver held rock-steady in a brown-skinned hand, the muzzle pointed at his head across the pommel of the young fellow's stock saddle. Bailey did not complete the draw; for some reason, a faint shine of moisture appeared on his cheeks, that slowly lost some of their color.

He found words, that were tight with emotion. "You dare to draw on me?"

"You seemed to insist," the other said in a toneless voice. "Maybe you'd like to get down out of that saddle and pick up that stuff you dumped, yourself."

"You'd have to shoot me first!" the non-com snarled, fury heating up his eyes.

"All right, then move on and give the old

man a chance to do it. He won't, long as you're hovering over him and he don't know what to expect next." The black eyes touched the other pair of troopers, including them. "Haven't you had your fun?"

For a long moment nothing happened. The troopers were waiting for their sergeant to give them a cue; he, for his part, was intently studying the impassive face of the man with the gun. Finally, Bailey's chest swelled within his sweated tunic and he took his hand from the holstered weapon and picked up the reins. But before he turned his mount he demanded gruffly, "How do they call you?"

"Logan, John Logan."

The mouth beneath the sandy mustache twisted in a sneer. "What the hell is an Injun doing, wearing a white man's name?"

But this time his only answer was that same unwavering stare. He shrugged, deliberately turning his back on the gun, and gave the reins a vicious yank that brought the horse around sharply. His two companions shared a look; without further words they sent their animals after him. They rode off in the direction of the trading post, not looking back.

Johnny Logan let the trapped breath from his lungs, and eased down the hammer of the gun; but he held it a moment longer, uneasily watching the backs of the blue-clad riders—remembering the promise of violence that had looked at him out of the sergeant's hot stare. Only when he was satisfied that Bailey had actually accepted his defeat did he finally slide the revolver back into its holster. And then the voice of the old Indian, speaking to him, brought his attention back to the one he'd rescued.

The old fellow was on his feet, now, and he was standing close to Johnny Logan's horse and talking rapidly, his hands moving in gestures as fluent as his tongue, his head tilted back and the long, graying hair sweeping the shoulders of a faded calico shirt. Johnny listened respectfully, but to no use. He could make nothing of the strange speech, that to his untrained ear seemed to run together in one unbroken flow of gutturals and consonants; he did, once or twice, seem to make out the word "*tsis-tsis-tas*," which he knew was the name by which the Cheyennes called themselves—"the People." But in the end he had to smile and shake his head, bringing the outpour of language to a halt.

"Sorry, old man," he said gently. "I can't talk with your tongue."

The brows drew down into a fierce scowl; the red-rimmed eyes peered up at him with suspicion. In uncertain English the man said, "You're not of the People? You not Indian—from the Reservation?"

"Far as I know," Johnny explained carefully,

"I'm a full-blood Cheyenne. But that's just about all I *do* know. My family was killed too long ago for me to remember."

"And you not from the Reservation?" the old man said for the second time, as though trying to sort things out and get them straight in his own slow thoughts.

Johnny Logan shook his head. "I've never even been there." He looked again to see what had become of the troopers, but they had vanished from sight beyond the log structure that housed the trading post; for the time being he decided to forget about them. "Let me help you with this stuff," he said, and stepped from his saddle to pick up the gunny sack.

The old man snatched it from him and set to work gathering the pitiful things Sergeant Bailey had scattered. Johnny Logan shrugged and stood by to watch him work. Thinking of the sergeant, he said gruffly, "He's not the first bully I've run across. A man like that will hurt anything he thinks can't hit back."

Not answering, the old man finished reloading his skimpy belongings into the sack, and flipped it into place onto a shoulder that was bowed and rounded with time.

"Despite what the man said," Johnny commented, "about not drinking trade whiskey, I'll wager what he was really after was some free likker he could confiscate for himself."

The Indian shook his head, the lank gray strands brushing his collar. "No whiskey," he repeated doggedly. And without another word, or any thanks for what the other had done, he turned and started away at a jogging trot—knees lifted high, moccasined toes turned in as he trotted away along an obscure footpath that led into the trees.

Johnny Logan, more amused than anything at the man's bristly manner, watched him go until the shadow of the pines swallowed him up. Turning then, he got the stirrup and swung astride the black; but he did not ride on toward the cross-roads and the trading post. Instead, frowning thoughtfully, he sat a moment considering the direction the old man had taken. On an impulse, he sent his animal after him, at an easy walk.

He went through the trees, hearing a sound of water, and came out on the bank of a shallow, clear-flowing stream that must, farther down, supply the trading post. Here, a shanty of sorts had been constructed on the bare mud above the creek's bank; it had been made of packing cases and logs and dirt, with a roof fashioned from flattened tins, and a slab of boards nailed together that apparently could be placed over the door opening. Johnny would have had to stoop nearly double to negotiate the entrance; the interior, without windows, was too dark to give him any idea how the tiny structure was furnished, if at all. The mud was littered with trash; on a rack of peeled poles lashed together with rawhide, an animal skin of some sort was drying.

The old Indian squatted in the mud beside his door, the gunny sack lying beside him. He peered sharply from under his brows as Johnny rode up to a halt.

"You live here?" Johnny said. "You like this better than the Reservation?"

The fierce eyes flashed with contempt. "Stands Talking no Reservation Indian!"

"Even if it means living all alone, cut off from your people?" But Johnny Logan quickly added: "Well, that's your affair; I certainly don't mean to argue a thing that's none of my business. I only wondered if I could talk to you for a little— something I'd like to show you, and ask you about."

He waited for his answer. The horse stomped and tossed its head, as though it didn't like the smell of this crude camp on the streambank. Johnny had about decided the old man would never unbend enough to invite him to step down; but perhaps Stands Talking was capable of a kind of gratitude, after all, toward this stranger who had rescued him from the hands of the troopers. For he shrugged his narrow shoulders, an indifferent gesture which Johnny Logan interpreted as permission to do whatever he liked. Swinging down, he knotted the black's reins to a pine branch a little distance away, and came back and went down beside the old Indian, squatting on his heels near the entrance to the jimcrack shanty.

Stands Talking gave his guest a sly, sidelong look, and reached into his clothing and from somewhere brought out a flat bottle nearly filled with poisonous-looking liquid. Johnny stared at it. "So!" he grunted. "The sergeant *was* right, after all!"

The old man gave a cackling laugh as he pulled the cork with his yellow teeth. He offered the bottle to his visitor but the latter shook his head, face expressionless. So Stands Talking put the bottle to his own lips and tossed his head back, and his Adam's apple worked as he ran the cheap whiskey into his throat.

He lowered the bottle, and giggled; but this time the laugh turned into a fit of painful coughing as some of the fiery stuff went down the wrong way. It turned him helpless, bent over, shoulders shaking. And Johnny seized the chance to take the bottle from his unresisting hand, and place it carefully to one side where the old man was not apt to see it. Then he waited while Stands Talking rode out the spasm, blindly, with whiskey and saliva running from his mouth. At last the old man got control, and scrubbed a wrist across his mouth, and palmed the streaming tears from red-rimmed eyes. When he started peering about, as though hunting the bottle, the other spoke quickly in an effort to distract him.

"I started to tell you," he said, "my name's Logan. At least, that's the white man's name I was raised by, from the time I was a baby. I never knew my real name—had no chance to know my own people at all. But I've been told they were Cheyenne."

As he hoped, Stands Talking seemed to have forgotten about the liquor. He was peering closely at the stranger, a scowl on his wrinkled face. "White man steal?"

"No, no," Johnny corrected him. "I wasn't stolen—my people were killed. All of them. I don't know how many there were; four or five lodges, I understand. It happened some eighteen years ago, over toward the foothills of the Bitterroots. I've been told there was bad sickness among the tribes that summer, and this group had gone west hoping to get away from it.

"But they ran afoul of some white ranchers who didn't like them camped so close to their beef herds. A bunch got drunk, and attacked the camp, without giving the slightest warning. It turned into a massacre. They killed everyone— men, women, children . . ." Johnny Logan's voice was bleak as he told of it. He paused, closely watching the other's face when he added, "As I say, that happened eighteen years ago. I just wondered if it might ring a bell with you."

But the opaque black eyes showed no glimmer of recognition. Johnny Logan was disappointed, though not surprised; on a raw frontier such as Montana had been eighteen years ago, the massacre of a few Indians had been a very minor incident. The whites who committed it would have said little about it afterwards, and none of the victims had escaped to carry the tale back to their own people. In this month of searching, Johnny's discreet questions had so far drawn nothing but blanks; he had really expected no better luck with the old Cheyenne.

He had set the old man off, though, into a long and angry tirade in the tongue that meant nothing to Johnny. He waited patiently for a good moment to break in, and then he said gently, "I've told you already, I only know a word or two of your language. I was too little to remember the Indian way of life at all. After they'd finished killing, the white men set fire to the lodges— burned everything to the ground and left. But a rancher named Matt Logan had got wind, too late, of what was afoot. He rode there as fast as he could, to stop it, but I was the only one still alive—though I'd been shot, too, like all the rest. He picked me up and took me home with him. He and his wife had just lost a youngster, to summer complaint. They adopted me in his place—took me in and raised me, exactly as though I'd been their own. I never left—until a month ago after Matt Logan died . . ."

He stopped. Stands Talking was no longer listening; his watery eyes were peering about, searching, and Johnny Logan knew he was hunting for the bottle. Johnny heaved a sigh of exasperation; in an attempt to distract the old fellow's attention he said quickly, "I told you I had something I wanted you to look at. All right?" And from a pocket of his shirt he took a small object.

It was a pouch, made of pliant doeskin that had begun to harden and turn dark with age, obviously made to be worn about the throat of its owner on a rawhide thing that was now missing. It was about the size to cover a man's palm, and it had molded itself with time to the shape of whatever mysterious objects had long ago been sewn into it by the rawhide stitching about its edges—Johnny had made no attempt to open it, and he never meant to. Stands Talking had put out a gnarled hand but when he saw what Johnny held he quickly snatched it back; scowling fiercely he said, "Medicine bag," and shook his head. "Bad . . ."

"To handle someone else's magic?" Johnny interpreted. "I guess I can understand that. In my own case, though, I have an idea it's all right because I think this belonged to my father. At least the man who wore it was holding me in his arms, when they found us; he had been killed trying to protect me. Matt Logan took this off his body, thinking someday I might want to have it—the only thing I would ever own that belonged to any of my people.

"But here's what I really wanted to ask you about . . ."

He turned the pouch over. It bore markings, the pigment faded by time but still faintly visible on the darkened leather: an arrow broken in two, a cloud with jagged lightning jutting beneath its flat bottom edge. But the central area was taken up by the tiny figure of a bear. Though it was only hinted at, its few deft lines were astonishingly effective: When you looked closely you could see that the animal was rearing, the sharp teeth bared, one forepaw raised to strike. . . .

"This is the only clue I have," Johnny Logan said, as the old Indian frowned over the markings. "The bear may stand for my father, in some way. Anyhow, in these last few weeks I've ridden a lot of miles and I've talked to a lot of people. I've been shown all kinds of paintings, on war shields and lodges and I don't know what-all; but compared to this they mostly looked like daubs. I don't know who did this. It might have been my father himself; or it might have been someone else—I suppose the bag could even have been made, and decorated, by two different people. But I *am* sure there can't

19

have been very many men with this sort of skill."

Stands Talking said nothing. He rubbed his nose with a gnarled forefinger, gazing at the creek as though he had no intention of speaking again. And Johnny Logan shrugged and said, "Well, I'm sorry to have bothered you—but I've got so I never pass up a chance. Maybe it wouldn't seem important to anyone else. On the other hand—" and his voice turned a little grim "—maybe it might, if he'd been raised among white men who never let him forget for a minute that he wasn't one of them . . . if he felt like he'd been grabbed out of his own world and put into another, where he doesn't belong . . ."

He got to his feet. And then Stands Talking, without rising or moving his head, said something in his own tongue that was completely meaningless to Johnny Logan. "You'll have to speak English," Johnny reminded him again.

"Lame Elk," the old man said, as though translating. It sounded like a name; he confirmed this as he slanted a rheumy glance up at the tall young man standing beside him. "Him maybe make picture . . ."

Johnny felt a first stirring of excitement. "And who's Lame Elk?"

"Old time medicine man of the *tsis-tsis-tas*. Make pictures that talk. Like that one."

"You're sure? You've seen them yourself?"

The old man nodded, greasy hair dragging across his shoulders. Johnny Logan demanded, "Where can I find this man?"

But to that question, Stands Talking shrugged. "Dead."

"Oh . . ."

Swift disappointment crowded in as the other continued: "Lame Elk was old man when Stands Talking tall and strong—young, like Johnny Logan."

"But he *might* still be alive. How many years since you actually saw or heard of him?" Stands Talking merely lifted his shoulders—it was maddening to try and drag information out of the man. Johnny Logan swallowed his impatience; he took a breath. "Would there be someone—some place—that I could ask and maybe learn something definite, either way?"

The old man seemed to consider, behind the gnarled thickets of his brows; Johnny wanted to shake him. Finally the Indian said, "You go Reservation?"

"That's where I was headed. Why? You think there could be people there, still living, who might tell me about this Lame Elk? Or recognize his work—maybe even remember the man this bag was made for?"

But the other only shrugged again, so that the gnarled hands flopped loosely on their wrists. "Dunno," he grunted, squinting at the sun-sparkles on the water. "Long time ago. All dead—all dead but Stands Talking . . ."

Plainly he had no more to say, but this much was something—the first hint of any kind that the search might bring results. Johnny Logan nodded, and tucked the medicine bag away into the pocket of his shirt. "Thanks," he said gruffly.

He walked to his horse, freed the reins and mounted. The old Indian had not moved, or spoken again. As he rode away through the trees, toward the trading post, the last sight Johnny had of him was his bent and motionless figure, squatting in front of the shanty and staring at the hypnotic slide of the blue-brown, swirling creek.

CHAPTER II

The trading post, with its clutter of outbuildings, sat backed up to the stream-bank timber and facing the brown ribbon of wagon road that brought trade past its door. Toward the rear, someone was working in a lean-to smithy; the rhythmic sound of a maul striking cooling metal broke the stillness as Johnny drifted in.

His route took him past a single big pine that stood in the hoof-trampled area before the main building; he was quite close before he noticed, in the flickering shadows piled there by the high noon sun, a horse standing motionless, rein-tied to his trunk—a chestnut animal, under full gear and worn stock saddle. A couple of men were there as well, so absorbed in talk that they didn't notice Johnny until he was almost upon them. One, attired in denims and boots and a brown corduroy jacket and wide-brimmed hat, had the look of a rancher and probably owned the horse. And even before the other one jerked up his head to stare at the newcomer, breaking off in mid-sentence, Johnny Logan had seen the blue uniform, the yellow stripe along the pantleg, the chevrons that identified him as Sergeant Bailey.

By now, Johnny had sincerely hoped the troopers would have had time to be gone about their business—the last thing he wanted was more trouble, on account of his daring to interrupt their sport with the old Cheyenne. But the way the non-com glared at him, slowly turning his head as Johnny rode on toward the door of the trading post, was warning enough.

So be it. He certainly couldn't turn tail and run just because the sergeant gave him a hard look. He dismounted in front of the store-building, looped his reins across the porch railing. He climbed split-log steps, and walked in through the propped-open door.

The trading post was a clutter—canned goods on shelves, clothing and harness and rope hanging from nails, bins and tables overflowing with odds and ends of merchandise. A man was on his knees beside a wooden crate, using a crowbar to prize off the lid; a screech of protesting nails greeted Johnny and set his teeth on edge.

The trader saw he had a customer and he got to his feet with something of an effort—he was not a young man, and he appeared to favor a rheumatic left hip. Watery blue eyes passed casually over the stranger, reached his face and held there a moment in a way that was thoroughly familiar to Johnny.

At first glance people usually took him for an ordinary cowpuncher. The fact that he wore his coal-black hair nearly as short as a white man's helped to confuse strangers. They invariably showed the reaction when, at a second look, they saw the dark skin, the high cheekbones and strongly-arched nose that branded him a full-blood Indian.

"Something I can do for you?" the trader asked bruskly.

"I'm short a few things," Johnny told him. "Coffee, beans, bacon. I guess you carry such items?"

"It's why I'm in business," the man said. He was still holding the crowbar. He laid it atop the crate and Johnny followed him over to a counter, while the trader went behind it to get the things he wanted and set them out. Johnny added a small sack of flour to the order. He was asked, "You want these in a sack?"

"My horse is tied outside," he answered. "I'll just put them in the saddlebags. How much?" He fished up the price from his pocket, in silver cartwheels. As the trader made change from his cash drawer Johnny asked, "Can you give me directions to the Cheyenne Reservation?"

That got a curious look, as though the other man considered it a peculiar question; but he answered it: "Walker Springs Agency's about thirty miles north. The Reservation's a big one—takes five agencies to run it. But Walker Springs is the main one."

"Well, then I guess that's the one I want. Where do I pick up the trail?"

The trader pointed with his chin. "Just beyond the belt of trees yonder, where those aspen run up into the draw. There's a good road, north through the draw. You can see it from the door."

Johnny stepped over for a look. What he saw was that the conversation beneath the pine had ended. The second man was already in the saddle of his horse and riding away; and now Sergeant Bailey, swinging around, gave the trading post a look and started directly toward it. The length of his stride, the set of his heavy shoulders, told Johnny what was coming. He sighed and walked back to the counter.

He said, "I've changed my mind. I'll need that sack, after all. . . ."

The man found one under the counter and was stowing the packages of food into it, when the non-com's boots struck the porch. Wondering how the sergeant meant to begin, Johnny Logan turned slowly and put his back to the counter as Bailey came to a menacing stand, facing him a dozen steps away.

Out of the saddle, he was big enough—taller than Johnny, who was tall for a Cheyenne, and wider of frame; his heavy bones were hung with muscle. Barracks brawls had toughened him. Johnny's heart sank a little. He had a feeling that bad things were about to happen.

The sergeant's mean stare shuttled from the trader to his customer. He said loudly, "Spellman, you ain't got pride enough to care *who* you deal with, do you? Whether he's white, or a lousy stinkin' Injun!"

Spellman's aging features showed no expression. "One man's silver is as good as another's," he said coolly, and he rang one of the dollars Johnny had given him against the counter. Its chime sounded loud in the stillness.

The sergeant's scowl darkened. "But this red bastard pulled a gun on me!"

"And we both know why, don't we, Sergeant?" Johnny Logan said grimly. Deliberately he turned his back on the scowling non-com, and moved to pick up the sack containing his supplies. It was a gesture of dismissal.

Bailey was not a man to be put aside. He swore, luridly, and Johnny heard the thump of his boots as he strode forward; when the sergeant's heavy fist dropped upon his shoulder to haul him around, he was set for it. He spun, his shoulder dropping away from under the sergeant's grip. He put the momentum of his motion behind the fist that he drove, wrist-deep, into Bailey's wind.

The non-com was big and he was tough, but Johnny had already judged that his thick middle was apt to be a vulnerable point. Taken without warning, or a chance to tighten his diaphragm against the unexpected blow, Bailey got the full force of it. Johnny's fist seemed never to quit sinking in. He saw the piggish eyes, so close to his own, pop wide with agony and a sour gush of breath broke from the man's lips beneath the sandy mustache.

A little desperately, because he knew that he had to finish what he had started, he tried to follow up the brief advantage of that first blow by hurling his left fist at the bigger man's jaw; but the non-com moved aside and Johnny's knuckles bounced harmlessly off the heavy muscle of his shoulder. And then one of the sergeant's fists struck Johnny on the ear like a club, and his whole head rang.

The blow staggered him. For a second or two his vision darkened and his knees felt as though they had turned to rubber.

Bailey could have finished him at that instant, but the big man was still having trouble with his breathing and he must have held back a moment as he fought to fill his lungs. It was enough time for Johnny's head to clear; light and color swam back into the world, and he caught his footing before his knees could let him go down. And there was Bailey, looming over him and wading in now with those blocky fists working.

Head still ringing, Johnny Logan circled away. Growing up on a schoolyard where he was the only Indian lad among a crew of white boys, mostly older and bigger and completely intolerant, had taught him a lot about survival in a rough-and-tumble. Now he felt the edge of the counter at his back and knew at once he must not let himself be trapped there; he slid away before Bailey could close with him. Dimly he was aware of Spellman, the trader, shouting, "Bailey! Damn it, you wreck my place and I'll hold your major responsible for the damages. . . ."

The sergeant ignored him, and made his rush. Desperately, Johnny Logan ducked away as a looping fist swung at his head. Bailey had put all his bulk behind the blow and when it missed he was strung out, weight unevenly distributed on his boots. Johnny sensed the brief instant of advantage, and he knew he had to press it for as much as it was worth. Still easing away, he checked himself suddenly and instead moved directly inside the sweep of the man's flailing arm. He cocked a right and let Bailey's own momentum add weight to the blow, aimed at the hinge of the man's jaw.

His knuckles landed, with an aching impact; there was a distinct popping noise and Bailey's head was flung violently toward his right shoulder. The non-com's eyes fluttered; suddenly he was spilling down, to land heavily against a corner of the crate that Spellman had left sitting in the middle of the floor.

Johnny Logan caught himself and, breathing hard, stared down at the man he had felled. The sergeant wasn't out, but he was dazed. He lay sprawled, one arm across the top of the crate, his head wobbling. Johnny flexed his aching right hand, and as though from a distance heard Spellman's warning: "You best get out of here, if you don't want more! Ed Bailey don't like to get beaten, by any man—and he dearly hates Indians!"

"I noticed that," Johnny Logan said, nodding woodenly. He had lost his hat during the brief fight; he leaned for it, and then stepped over to the counter and got his purchases. "And you're right," he told Spellman. "I didn't ask for this— and I don't want any more." He looked again at the sergeant, who was making uncertain movements as he recovered from that last blow. Bailey got a hand under him and pushed up toward a sitting position; but the arm gave way and let him sprawl back against the edge of the crate.

Johnny Logan turned his back and walked to the door, his sack of supplies under one elbow.

He was nearly there when he heard the trader's warning shout behind him. Halting, he turned just in time to see Bailey's arm snap and the crowbar, that he'd snatched up from the top of the crate where Spellman had left it, come spinning at his head in a dull blur of steel. There was not too much force behind the throw; he had time enough to step aside and let the bar streak past his shoulder, to clatter against the wall. He gave the man who had thrown it a single contemptuous look, and then deliberately turned his back on him.

Dropping down a couple of plank steps to where his horse was tied, Johnny slung his bag of supplies across the pack that was strapped behind the cantle of his saddle. As he did he saw the pair of troopers who had been with Sergeant Bailey just coming into view from the rear of the trading post, leading their horses—they were the ones, he supposed, that he'd heard working in the smithy when he first rode up. Johnny kept an eye on them, but chiefly he was listening for sound within the building as he reached to free the reins.

In the next moment, a heavy tramp of boots all but shook the porch; Ed Bailey came storming out, looking for the man who had put him down. At the edge of the steps he halted, catching sight of Johnny below him with the black's reins in his hand. He flung out an arm and shouted, "You red sonofabitch! I'll break you in two!"

"No you won't!" Johnny Logan answered crisply, and moved his body so that Bailey could see the revolver he had slid from its holster. The sergeant, blinded by rage, may not even have noticed it. He started down the steps; Johnny, determined not to let this come hand-to-hand a second time, lowered the weapon and deliberately squeezed off a shot, putting the bullet into the step just below Bailey's foot. The report cracked flatly, beating sharp echoes off the front of the trading post. Ed Bailey caught himself and quickly withdrew the reaching boot. And Johnny Logan tilted the smoking muzzle so that it pointed squarely at the non-com's thick chest.

As though just remembering he had a pistol in his own holster, the sergeant started to put a hand on it. He thought better of that and dropped his arm, and stood there glaring at the gun and at the one who held it. His face had gone a little white, suddenly; there was a red smear across one cheek where Johnny's knuckles had broken the skin. A hoarse, scarcely human sound came from him.

Johnny Logan, during all this time, was well aware of the other troopers and now he shifted position slightly, so that he could look across his saddle to pick them up. They had come to a halt, staring; he called sharply, "Don't either of you move! This is between me and your sergeant."

And then his head whipped around, as he became aware of still another horseman approaching the trading post.

This one, too, was a cavalryman—but an officer, wearing the neat uniform and the gold leaves of a major. Apparently he had just arrived, following the wagon road out of the timber, but the keen interest he seemed to show in what was happening here warned Johnny that he, and these other horse soldiers, probably belonged together.

He drew rein and suddenly Johnny found himself uncomfortably boxed, with the major on his left and the pair of troopers an equal distance to the right of him. The officer told him sharply, "I don't know what's going on here—but you better put away that gun if you don't want trouble."

"I don't want trouble, Major," Johnny Logan answered, not moving to obey the order. "But this man's jumped me once already. I'm not going to let him do it again."

"Sergeant Bailey is under my command," the officer said coldly. "I'll be responsible for him. Now, put up the gun!"

There was a tense moment as Johnny hesitated. The trader Spellman came out, joining Bailey on the porch. The two troopers from the blacksmith shed had still not shifted position. Then, reluctantly, Johnny lowered the hammer of the weapon and dropped it back into its holster.

At once Ed Bailey seemed to break free of the trance that had held him since the bullet drove into the boards beneath his feet. Seeing there was no longer a gun pointed at him, he gave a bellow and started down the steps, again, making for Johnny Logan; it took a second sharp command from the major to get through to him. "Sergeant! I want this stopped. Now!"

Bailey halted, but the look he swung toward the major held pure disdain. To Johnny, the officer seemed a man of authority and yet a little out of place—a desk soldier, perhaps, transferred to the saddle. His cleanshaven features were a trifle fleshy, and until recently he didn't appear to have been out in the weather very much; by contrast to the darkened skins of the troopers, his face and the backs of his hands were sunburned and peeling. That might be enough in itself to make a toughened, line non-com like Bailey look on him with something bordering on contempt.

"The man's a troublemaker, Major," he said roughly. "He's got a lesson coming to him."

"I'll decide that!" the other snapped, and looked again at Johnny Logan. "You'd better have a good reason, for pulling a weapon on a non-commissioned officer of the United States Cavalry!"

"I just wanted him to let me alone," Johnny answered. "As for what started the trouble, he and these two"—he indicated them with a nod—"were abusing an old Indian, a harmless sort of fellow who lives in a shanty on the creekbank. I watched it as long as I could and finally cut in and made them stop. And they didn't seem to like it."

"That would be Stands Talking," the trader put in. The major looked at him.

"Are you a witness to the incident?"

"No, I didn't happen to see it. But the old fellow *is* harmless—I'll vouch for that. He's a Cheyenne, too proud to live on the Reservation. He does odd jobs for me, fishes a little, does

34

some trapping and trades me the pelts. . . ."

The officer turned to his sergeant. "Were you abusing him?"

"Hell!" Ed Bailey shrugged heavy shoulders. "Just having a little fun, was all. No reason for this red-skinned sonofabitch to put his horn in!"

"I see?" The major's pale stare returned to Johnny Logan's face, rested there as though puzzling out something; suddenly he said, "Am I mistaken, or are you an Indian yourself?"

"You're not mistaken," Johnny agreed shortly.

"And that would be the reason you felt obliged to interfere. . . ."

"Part of the reason, I guess."

"I see," the officer repeated. He seemed to reach a decision, then.

"Well, there seems no real harm done. We'll forget it. But I suggest you get in that saddle and go on about your business."

It was a curt dismissal, but Johnny Logan was glad enough to see an end to this on any terms. He hadn't backed down to the tough sergeant; he had held his own and even done a little better, and he could not see that he had anything to be ashamed of if he obeyed the major's order now. He jerked the reins free, found stirrup and lifted to his saddle. On the steps, Ed Bailey watched with a thunderous look, his mean eyes full of hatred.

Without another word Johnny Logan turned

the black and rode away, eastward through the shallow valley. He went without hurry, but he felt the stares that followed him; just before the trail turned into some trees he looked back, and they were all looking after him; Bailey had an arm raised to touch the sleeve to his cheek where Johnny's fist had drawn blood.

Johnny felt more relieved than he liked to admit, when that scene fell away behind him.

He found the branch-off of the Reservation road easily enough, nothing more than a set of wagon ruts that left the main trail and eased up through the draw the trader had pointed out to him. Once free of the creek bottom, it looped northward and eastward across the dips and rolls of a grassland turned brown with summer, with a low running line of mountains blue in the distance and the sky like a wide dome. A man felt small, under that cloud-dotted sky; to match it, he had to grow almost larger than life—it was a thing you came to notice about Montana men.

Another thirty miles . . . Tomorrow should bring him to the Reservation and perhaps—if he was lucky—to the end of the trail that the little bag, with the bear and its other painted symbols, had led him. Or, perhaps, merely to another blind alley. He supposed he'd known from the start he would be coming here eventually; he'd been working more or less steadily in this direction, and might have spared himself weeks of delay over fruitless inquiries made along the route. But he thought he knew why he had deliberately taken his time.

After all, the Reservation meant his last real hope. There, among the Northern Cheyenne, was the one place he might find the clue he was hoping for—to his origins, and his people. If not, then he knew he might as well give it up. . . .

After a while, in a pause to let the black drink from a shallow stream, he dismounted and transferred the things he had bought at the trading post to the saddlebags where he kept his supplies. And it was then, as he stood looking about him in the quiet of the empty land, he caught the first hint of movement on the trail behind him.

He went still, instantly cautious. Those other travelers were still too far away to notice him, against a neutral background of rock and scrub, so he stood and watched until a dark clot of figures separated itself into the outlines of four horsemen, riding two and two.

Then, leading the black, he took to the rounded pebbles of the streambed and followed its meanders away from the trail crossing to where a screen of wild rose bushes offered concealment. Here he waited, listening to a silence that was complete except for the sound of the wind combing the grass and the brush, the buzz of a fly, the chuckle of the stream over its stones.

It was a tedious business. These horsemen were in no great hurry, and a good part of an hour had dragged out before Johnny could make out the thud of hoofs and jingle of gear, and a hum of voices that told him the riders were getting close. He got a hold on the black's headstall, ready to cut off any betraying whicker of greeting.

Abruptly, the noise of hoofs ceased.

Very cautiously disturbing a branch of wild rose bush, he peered out and saw that the four troopers, without dismounting, had halted to let their mounts drink; the murmur of their talk reached him only faintly. Next to the major, Ed Bailey was scowling silently at the stream in a way that made Johnny Logan uneasily aware of the sign he must have left when he led his horse into cover.

But if the sign was there, no one appeared to see it. Presently the officer gave a command; the sergeant fell in beside him, the other two taking their places at the rear. They rode on, and the flow of the land swallowed them up.

Johnny Logan was left frowning, unhappy about this. He didn't suppose they could actually be following him; what he didn't like was being on the same trail, heading in the same direction—though he did feel better not to have them behind him.

But it meant they could only be going one place, which happened to be Johnny's own destination: the sprawling Cheyenne Reservation. And he didn't relish the thought that he might have to face another confrontation with the cruel-eyed, Indian-hating sergeant.

CHAPTER III

The Northern Cheyenne appeared to have been luckier than most, in the reservation lands assigned them. Unlike so many others, shunted onto miserable tracts of waste that no white man wanted, Johnny Logan understood their leaders had been allowed pretty much to make the choice for themselves—and at a time when this section of Montana was still almost free of settlement. They'd chosen well. He liked the country he saw: pine-covered hills that looked as though they should be rich in game, with sparkling streams, and good grass for the horses that were the measure of an Indian's wealth.

The Cheyenne, of course, had had to forfeit their old, nomadic way of life; but on the other hand, Johnny knew that as wards of the Government they were given rations and farming tools, clothing and supplies of many kinds. Even if a fiercely independent old man like Stands Talking was too proud to move onto the Reservation, or take the white-eyes' charity, for others it did seem reasonable to think there might be compensations.

He frankly didn't know; he intended to find out.

Following the wagon road this last distance

into the agency at Walker Springs, it was close to noon when he finally brought it in sight. He had hardly known what he expected; what he saw was an extensive group of log buildings, set against a protecting ridge. There were sheds and outbuildings, a warehouse and other structures, a small cluster of canvas tepees. In front of the main building, a United States flag on a tall pole tugged and snapped in the wind.

The thing Johnny Logan really wasn't prepared for, was the busy activity of the place.

Ponies and wagon teams stood at their tie ropes, all about the work area, with more arriving on the trails that convened upon the agency headquarters like the spokes of a wheel. Mining groups of humanity made a blur of color and a hum of sound, punctuated by shouting children and barking dogs. It was a special occasion, surely, and he puzzled over it until the obvious answer occurred to him: He must have got here on ration day.

The nearer he rode, the more certain he was. But it also made him uneasy. He was very much on the lookout for the troopers who had passed him on the trail, yesterday; he had purposely killed time, to avoid overtaking them and risking more trouble with the tough sergeant. He had camped early, using the supplies obtained at Spellman's. But if the agency had been their destination they might very well still be here.

And though he searched for some trace of a blue uniform, or a horse with a McClellan saddle, he knew the chances weren't good of spotting either, in that swarm about the agency buildings.

His gun was in a pocket of his saddlebags since he felt it wouldn't be a good idea to wear it openly. He thought about digging it out and strapping it on, then shook his head—that would be asking for trouble.

There was further activity around a bank of corrals that were set some distance below the buildings. Drifting nearer, he tried to discover just what was going on. Here, there were only men and older boys; among the Indians, he thought he spotted several who looked like white cowpunchers. He saw, too, that the pens contained some three dozen head of cattle, milling and bawling and raising dust.

There was a sudden flurry of action. A gate was flung open; men tumbled over themselves to clear the space in front of it. And out of the corral, a steer burst—head down, hoofs pounding the earth as the yells of cowboys lining the fence urged it to a flat-out run. In the same breath, a horse and rider exploded from the crowd and took after the animal. The rider—slim, muscular, naked except for moccasins and breechclout and headband—rode bareback, clamping the horse's barrel with his knees so as to leave his hands free. Johnny saw with admiration how his movements blended to those of the pony. Black hair streaming, he placed his mount beside and a little behind the running steer and they came pounding on together, almost directly toward the spot where Johnny Logan had reined in to watch.

The Indian held a bow, and there was a quiver of arrows slung over his shoulders; now he drew one and notched it to the rawhide string, drawing careful aim. But just as he released the shaft, his pony swerved; the arrow struck the steer's tough hide at an angle, and bounced off harmlessly. Without a wasted moment the brave readied another arrow, in a smooth blur of motion that Johnny Logan could scarcely believe. It leaped from the string; and this time the point drove home, unerringly, just behind the shoulder.

It struck deep, to the lungs and heart; momentum carried the steer forward another half dozen lunging steps and then, directly in front of Johnny Logan, it broke and plunged headlong, raising an explosion of dust. The head flopped, the legs threshed and twitched and the animal went motionless, with the arrow's feathered shaft standing between its ribs.

The black snorted and danced uneasily, until Johnny calmed it. All at once he understood what he had just witnessed. He could see the carcasses of a half dozen other steers lying where they had been dropped, bristling with more arrows—one big steer was pinioned by an ash wood lance.

Once these young men, or their fathers, had ridden to make meat from the great buffalo herds that were the mainstay of the Indian's economy. Now the buffalo had vanished, wiped out by the thundering rifles of white hide hunters who had swept the plains clear, like a plague of locusts. Their freedom gone, their livelihood gone, perhaps it was only in this manner—on ration day— that young Cheyenne braves could have, for a brief moment, experience of a way of life that was no more.

Over at the corral, the cowpunchers were at work getting the next steer cut out and ready to send through the gate. They plainly took the thing as a hilarious joke; Johnny Logan heard their laughing, and something about the whole pathetic farce drew his mouth down hard. And then he saw that the young brave who shot the steer was kicking his pony toward him and shouting in Cheyenne, his manner bristling with anger.

Johnny could only shake his head and tell him, as he had told Stands Talking, "Sorry. I only know English."

The young fellow reined in, scowling. Loudly he said, "In English, then: You make fun of Swooping Hawk?"

"I don't know where you got that idea," Johnny said. "I wasn't making fun of anybody."

"You laugh, because I miss my first arrow!"

Swooping Hawk was directly in front of Johnny, blocking the road. He was about Johnny's age—perhaps in his early twenties. His coppery body shone with healthy perspiration: his flat lips writhed with fury. The bow he clenched in upraised fist was a handsome one, its ends tipped with horn and fluttering with eagle feathers.

"You think you do better?" He leaned to shake the bow under Johnny's nose. "Take Swooping Hawk's own weapon—take Swooping Hawk's arrows. Show us!"

Over the hubbub at the pen, one of the cowboys yelled loudly, "All right, which of you mighty warriors wants to run this next buffalo?" Looking coldly into Swooping Hawk's furious black eyes, Johnny found himself thinking, *You're too proud to be made fun of—but you make a laughing stock of yourself for those cowpunchers!*

Instead of saying this, he shook his head and told the young Indian, "There'd be no contest at all. I've never pulled a bow in my life." And he walked the black around the other's pony, and rode on.

Swooping Hawk was not to be put off. At once he was after Johnny, crowding him, hurling taunts: "You—white Indian!" The words dripped with contempt. "You wear the white-eye's clothing—you talk his language—you sneer at the ways of the People. But the brave white Indian turns from Swooping Hawk's challenge.

The white Indian has the heart of a rabbit!"

By this time they had nearly reached the pens. And now anger had its way with Johnny Logan. He reined in, turning his head sharply to look at the other's contorted face. He started to make a hot reply, saw the futility of that. His jaw firmed; he looked around toward the men at the corral.

They were still waiting to turn loose the steer they had cut out and were holding against the gate, with prods and slapping ropes. Johnny saw this was a big fellow—there was the glint of wicked horns as it tossed its head, and snorted in terror and dug at the earth with sharp hoofs.

With a sudden decision Johnny lifted an arm. He shouted across the dust: "Whenever you're ready. Let him go!"

He had time only to tug his hatbrim down firmly, settle himself in the leather; then the gate swung back and, amid the whoops of the cowboys, the big steer exploded into the open.

The black had been trained to this business by Johnny, himself. It hardly needed the touch of the spur; with the instinct of a cow horse it leaped forward and dropped into a run, at an angle that would bring it in shoulder to shoulder with the racing steer. Johnny Logan dropped the tied reins and shifted position, leaning and ready.

For this maneuver a rider had to come in dangerously close—much closer than had been necessary in order for Swooping Hawk to drive his arrow home. Johnny knew a slip, or a stumble, could hurl him directly onto the wicked points of the horns that bobbed just below him in time to the headlong rush over blurring ground. He caught the timing, judged his distances. And at the precise, correct instant, he launched himself from the saddle.

His reaching hands found the slick horns, clamped hard. His bootheels struck the earth and dug for purchase as he wrestled with the muscular, straining brute, and dust rose chokingly about them. Gradually he brought the animal to a stand; he got his boots set, but for a breathless moment—his muscles popping with effort, the blood pounding in his ears—he thought he was not going to be able to get the brute's head over.

Slowly, slowly, the steer gave to the twisting weight on its horns. Johnny bore it down until the bellowing wind of its nostrils dug furrows in the dust; even so, the animal's hoofs remained braced and it seemed its neck would snap before it yielded to the pressure.

With a thud that shook the ground, the heavy body whipped over. The animal struggled briefly, then lay quiet.

Johnny could feel its sides heave, as he caught his own breath before attempting the risky business of freeing those murderous horns. Carefully he got his knees under him, then in a single swift movement leaped up and back as the steer lumbered to its feet. But it did no more than throw him a resentful look, and trotted away swinging its head.

Johnny whipped dirt from his clothing with the flats of his hands. The black, like any good cow pony, had put on the brakes the instant he left its back, and was calmly nibbling the grass close by; Johnny caught the stirrup and swung aboard. And as he reined back toward the pens, he came face to face once more with Swooping Hawk.

The brave sat his pony, motionless, black eyes boring into him. Johnny knew the fellow would have to admit that what he had just witnessed called for even greater daring and risk than his own exploit with bow and arrow—and, in its way, an equal amount of skill. There was no need to labor the point. He simply touched his horse with the spur and rode past without a word.

Many eyes were watching him. As he came even with the white cowhands perched on the corral fence, one hailed him. "So you *are* an Injun! I couldn't rightly believe it! That's as neat a job of 'dogging as I ever seen."

"You never learned that trick here on the Reservation," a second puncher said.

"No," Johnny admitted. They seemed friendly enough so he explained: "There were some pretty fair bulldoggers in the crew on Star Ranch where I was raised."

"Star?" the first man repeated. "In the Bitter-roots? That's the Logan outfit, ain't it?"

Johnny nodded. He looked through the bars at the thirty-odd head of beef milling inside. They all bore the same mark—a Bar J. "You ride for this brand?"

The man said, "That's right—for Arne Jenson, over west of the Reservation. He's been supplying the beef ration here at Walker Springs, for the past couple of years."

Probably a fairly profitable contract for the rancher named Jenson, Johnny thought—a steady market for a certain number of head each month. While few of the animals in the pen could promise to dress out much in the way of fancy steaks, for the restaurant trade, they looked to have fair meat on them. Knowing the way a white rancher's mind worked, Johnny Logan imagined it could have been a temptation to fill the contract with stunted, underweight culls, or perhaps troublemakers—tough steers like the one Johnny had nailed, that would be too much to handle in a regular drive to a delivery point. Under the circumstances, he thought the Cheyenne were not being dealt with too badly by their supplier.

He said so, and the one who had done most of the talking agreed. "Jenson's a pretty honest fellow to deal with." He added, squinting thoughtfully at his questioner, "And you seem like a pretty good judge of beef cattle."

Johnny Logan shrugged. "Like I said, I was raised with them." He let it go at that, with a nod as he rode on toward the main buildings of the agency. Behind him there was a new burst of yelling and drumming of hoofs as one more ration steer was turned loose, so that another brave could practice the soon-to-be-forgotten skills of the great buffalo hunts—and the Bar J cowhands could laugh and whoop and egg him on.

To Johnny it seemed both debasing and pathetic. . . .

As he approached the buildings he picked his way carefully, searching faces and avoiding the youngsters who ran about almost under the hoofs of his horse. He supposed anyone who could fill out the little that Stands Talking had been able to tell him about the man called Lame Elk would have to be of an older generation than most of these—perhaps, someone at least as old as Stands Talking, himself. He noticed one fantastically wrinkled squaw, standing beside a wagon wrapped in her blanket despite the warmth of the summer day; but when he smiled and nodded she gave him a hostile stare, and her face closed like a fist and she deliberately turned her back.

Nor was she, the only one. Riding on, Johnny felt the same suspicious withdrawal in most of the dark glances he met. Obviously, to these people there was something wrong about an Indian who dressed and carried himself in the manner of a white man. Here, among what should have been his own people—of his own race—he felt more uncomfortably out of place than ever before in his life.

And then it occurred to him that without an interpreter he would probably be unable to communicate with the older Cheyenne, since he couldn't speak a word of the tongue and chances were that they knew little English. It was a problem. Perhaps his best bet lay in appealing directly to the agent.

Accordingly he picked his way across the compound toward the agency buildings. As he did so, he noticed something else about these people. The kids ran around, like kids anywhere, shouting over intricate games of their own; and yonder at the corrals there were bursts of yelling as the young braves continued their slaughter of the beef ration. But here around the agency buildings, it seemed to him the atmosphere was subdued and somehow dispirited.

It bothered Johnny Logan.

Now there was activity at the shed-like structure Johnny took to be a warehouse. A number of young Indians were passing in and out, toting crates and piles of goods to long deal tables that had been set up outside its cavernous double doors—he gathered that the issue of rations was in preparation. A white man, coatless and wearing a string tie and alpaca sleeve supporters, was walking about overseeing the work and checking off a list fastened to a clipboard. Johnny rode over to him.

The man wasn't young. He had thinning gray hair and a sour look about him, and he glanced at Johnny with open irritation. "Just move on!" he ordered imperiously. "We're not ready yet."

His manner was not pleasant, but Johnny dismounted, holding the black's reins as he said, "I'm not here for rations—I don't live on the Reservation. I'm looking for the agent. Are you him?"

"No," the other answered, as curtly as before; he would be an underling, then—a clerk of some sort. "Sid Walsh is tied up in a meeting," he said, and he inclined his head toward the main building, behind its flagpole that was neatly set out in a circle of whitewashed stones. When Johnny followed his glance the clerk added hastily, "He don't want to be bothered." And before Johnny Logan could ask further questions he turned away, dismissing him, and walked back into the shed.

Left standing there, Johnny frowned and ran the rein-ends through his hand, angered and debating his next move. One of the Indian helpers came out carrying a stack of cheap-looking, undented black hats with round brims. He made a place for them on the table by elbowing aside other piles of goods; in doing so he dislodged a pile of blankets and they toppled to the ground. Unaware or indifferent, he went back into the warehouse. Johnny Logan stooped and picked up the fallen blankets.

Something made him take a closer look. He flipped back the corner of one, felt of the material. Eyes narrowing, he worked at it and had no difficulty at all in pulling the fibers apart between his fingers. He flipped through the entire stack, saw that they were all the same—flimsy, sleazily woven stuff, cheaply dyed. Setting the blankets aside, he ran a look over the other things on the table. There was a box of horn-handled knives; Johnny picked one out and found that the blade was insecurely set into the grip—ran a thumb along the edge of the blade and discovered that it had no edge, and that the badly tempered steel was probably incapable of holding one. He tossed the knife back into the box, his eyes smoldering.

And then he noticed some bags of flour piled on the ground, at the end of the table. The whole stack bore suspicious-looking stains, that could have come from being submerged in water; to his touch the top bag felt hard as a rock and when he started to lift it he caught the rancid odor of mildew. . . .

Someone cried harshly, "You! Get away from there!"

It was the clerk, back again—standing in the door of the shed, anger in his voice. "What do you think you're up to?"

Johnny Logan straightened. He said coldly, "I'm looking at the worthless junk you intend handing out to these people!"

"None of my doing," the clerk snapped. "I only issue what I'm given."

"Then I won't waste time with you!" Johnny said grimly. The bags of spoiled flour were too heavy to manage. Instead he snatched one of the sleazy blankets and turned back with it to his horse.

"Drop that!"

Paying no heed, Johnny Logan stepped into saddle and reined directly toward the agency headquarters.

CHAPTER IV

When he glanced back, he saw that a second man had appeared in the warehouse doorway—summoned, perhaps, by the clerk. The latter was gesturing excitedly; the other lifted his stare in Johnny's direction, and Johnny saw that he was Indian, though dressed in white man's jeans and boots and denim jacket. A single eagle's feather was stuck into his hatband. And Johnny noticed two other things: the gun and holster strapped about his middle, and the glint of something metallic fastened to his shirt.

A badge. It labeled him as a member of the agency's Indian police.

He started walking quickly after Johnny Logan. The latter kept going, not changing his horse's easy gait, and when he reached the main building he swung down, the blanket under his arm, and dropped the black's reins to anchor it in cowpony fashion. Beyond the screen, a hum of talk came out to him through the open door. Overhead, in the wind, the flag popped on its lanyards like a gunshot.

The policeman broke into a run now, and one hand was fumbling at his holster. Johnny Logan hesitated, reluctant to break in without ceremony on whatever serious business was afoot inside the office—he could hear someone saying angrily, "By God, in all the months I been supplying the beef for this agency, I ain't ever give anyone cause for complaint!" But the policeman was coming, badge flashing at every step, and his gun was out of the holster; and unless Johnny acted quickly he would be cut off. Determination firmed his jaw, and he yanked open the screen and entered.

All talk broke off, abruptly.

This was obviously the heart and nerve center of the agency—a big room, crudely equipped, with a puncheon floor and muslin ceiling and screened windows with wooden shutters. A space heater, cold now, sent a stovepipe angling out through a hole in the log wall. There was a roll-top desk and swivel chair, a number of other chairs, a littered table and a wooden cabinet in one corner, and on the wall, a map of the sprawling Cheyenne Reservation. At the back of the room a door led probably to living quarters.

As Johnny let the screen close against his heel, four men turned their heads to stare. The one at the desk would be the agent himself—Walsh, the clerk had called him: a man with heavy brows and burnsides, and a mouth like the thin slash of a knife. What rather took Johnny Logan aback was to see the major seated next to him and, perched on a corner of the table behind them, Sergeant Ed Bailey swinging one booted foot and peering at the intruder with a fierce intensity.

It was the fourth man who had been speaking when Johnny entered. A cattleman from the look of him, he had leaped up from his chair and was shaking a finger at the Army officer, and his wind-whipped, craggy features were red with fury. Finding himself interrupted, he scowled and slowly let the arm fall to his side.

The Indian agent slapped both hands down on the arms of his chair. "What is this?" he demanded harshly. "Hasn't it been made clear to you people, I won't have you charging in here without permission?"

Johnny's mouth hardened. With the sound of running boots drawing nearer each second, he knew he had little time to say what he intended to. He drew a breath.

"In the first place," he began, "I'm not a Reservation Indian."

"I've seen him before!" the sergeant broke in. There was a fresh scab on his cheek from Johnny's knuckles. "Walsh, he's a damn smart-aleck redskin that calls himself by a white man's name and goes around looking for trouble."

Sid Walsh said curtly, "He'll find it here, if he isn't careful!" And to Johnny: "Get out!"

At that moment the screen door was thrown open. Johnny moved quickly aside as the one with the badge strode in, scowling. He gestured with his drawn revolver. "You!" he told Johnny in a harsh guttural. "Come!"

Johnny Logan was too angry to care about a gun. "I'll say what I came for." He plucked the blanket from under his arm and shook it out in front of the agent. "I'll ask you to your face: Is *this* what you issue to the Cheyenne? Blankets you can poke a finger through—spoiled food—nothing that isn't worthless junk!" Angrily he flung the blanket to the floor. "Is *this* why they gave up their freedom? Signed away their hunting grounds, and agreed to take charity from the white man—"

At a flickering signal from the Indian agent's eyes, the policeman's hand fell onto Johnny's shoulder, hard enough to make him wince. Walsh said coldly, "All right—you've made your speech. Little Wolf, take him out of here."

"You heard," the guttural voice said in Johnny's ear. "Move!"

"Hold on a moment!"

Johnny was surprised—it was the major who spoke. As the policeman hesitated, Johnny Logan shrugged the hand off his shoulder. The officer was looking at him narrowly. "What is it you call yourself?"

Johnny told him.

"Well, Logan, you do seem to be a trouble-maker—as the sergeant says. Any Indian who behaves the way you do is not apt to last very long. But this one time, at least, you happen to be right!"

As he was speaking he leaned for the blanket Johnny had flung down; he worked at the fibers, easily pulling them apart. He shook his head. "I'm afraid this sort of thing is an old story on Indian reservations all over the West—it's what comes of putting these agencies into the hands of civilians, with too much authority and no effective supervision. Sooner or later they find ways to line their own pockets and they do it, at the Government's—and the Indians'—expense."

Walsh had been getting redder in the face, gripping the arms of his chair; Johnny Logan thought he was going to lash out at the major, but something—guilt, perhaps—made him hold his tongue, his mouth tightened to a grim, straight line across his narrow face.

"For your information," the officer told Johnny, ignoring the agent, "I've seen what's in the warehouse, and there's nothing can be done about that—the stuff's there; it's been vouchered and paid for and the Cheyenne will just have to make the best of it till it's used up. But you might be glad to know that there's finally going to be a change in procedure. As an experiment, the Army has been ordered to take Indian supply out of the hands of the civilian agents, and do the purchasing ourselves. It puts extra burden on us, and maybe it won't work; but it's going to be tried.

"I'm Major Harriman," he went on. "Of the Quartermaster Corps, stationed at Fort Dilson in this area. I've been handed the job of purchasing supplies, not only for the Cheyenne Reservation, but for the Crows as well; and I can tell you, from now on, there'll be no more traffic in sleazy and worthless goods!"

Walsh could hold back no longer. "I don't have to listen to this!" he shouted, his knuckles white on the arms of the chair. "I know the terms of my contract. And I've filled it to the letter."

"You've filled your own pockets," the major retorted. He tossed the offending blanket contemptuously aside. "Had these Indians of yours starved to death—or been driven to stage an uprising, that the Army would have had to put down—it wouldn't have meant anything to you, or all the crooked contractors that men like you have done your business with!"

"Are you including *me* in that, Major?" The one with the look of a cattleman had been waiting silently, still on his feet, letting the argument roll about him. Now he took up the attack again, where Johnny's entrance had interrupted him. "I'm gonna tell you one more time—it's a lie! Whatever deals may have been made, far as I'm concerned it was always strictly business. Because my ranch is nearest to the Reservation,

I was able to name a fair price for beef deliveries and I kept my bargain. In these two years I've heard no complaints about the beef ration—never once!"

Johnny Logan spoke up. "Major, I don't know this man—but if his name is Jenson, I was just looking at some of his cattle out in the corral. They looked all right to me . . . maybe not prime beef, for the big markets, but nothing you could fault."

That brought attention back to him. It was Sergeant Bailey who said, with an open sneer, "Now I suppose, you claim to be an authority on beef stock!"

Johnny looked at him coldly. "As a matter of fact," he said, "I do."

"And I don't see why you shouldn't take his word for it!" Arne Jenson was shouting at the major again. "If one of their own kind says the beef is all right, then you got no grounds at all to cancel me out!"

The officer's fleshy features had colored slightly, but he was adamant. "The decision's been made, Jenson—I told you that. McCord's bid is lower. I've checked his herd and found it satisfactory. I'm notifying him that he's been awarded the contract."

"If Nels McCord underbid me," Arne Jenson retorted hotly, "then the man's up to something! He can't hope to make a profit honestly. . . ."

But Harriman was no longer listening. The major slapped both hands on his knees and got to his feet, saying, "If I'm to reach Piping Rock Agency before sundown, I'll have to get started." He looked around for Ed Bailey. "Sergeant, tell your men to bring the horses."

Bailey slid off the table's edge. Johnny, watching him, saw the man hesitate and for some reason had an impression that Bailey wasn't ready to leave just yet. The sergeant rubbed a fist across his thick mustache and seemed to try to catch Walsh's eye with a side-long look. But the agent was glowering darkly at Major Harriman, and Bailey appeared to change his mind; he shrugged and went tramping out of the office, nearly brushing Johnny Logan out of the way with one heavy shoulder.

The agent, Walsh, was on his feet by this time. Major Harriman turned to give him a final warning: "If I only had the authority," he said coldly, "I'd fire you out of that job. Luckily for you, I don't. But you'd best watch your step! Give me an excuse and I'll use any pressure I can to get rid of you!"

Ignoring the man's hating stare, he turned then to Johnny Logan. "As for you, I'm still not sure I know what your game is. But you strike me as a smart young man. Perhaps too smart! You may learn yet that a really wise Indian is the one who knows his place—and keeps it!" He gave Johnny no time to answer but, drawing on his hat, followed his sergeant outside.

"Major!" The cattleman, Arne Jenson, still wanted to argue. He was after the officer at once, letting the screen door slam behind him. But when Johnny Logan, too, moved a step in that direction, he heard Walsh say sharply, "Not so fast!" In the same moment he felt something hard and round shoved into his ribs and knew it was the muzzle of Little Wolf's gun. The breath caught in his lungs.

Outside, Jenson was trying to make the major listen to him, but Harriman merely stood and rocked from heel to toe while he looked off at the blue mountains in the distance, paying no attention. At last the cowman gave up and, with a furious oath, turned to a bay that was tied to a hitching post nearby. He swung astride, jerked the animal's head around and went riding off toward the corrals at a fast clip. And minutes later, Sergeant Bailey and the troopers appeared, leading the major's horse.

It cost the officer some effort to haul his weight into the saddle. He settled himself, and spoke an order; his command fell into their usual riding order and trotted away, heading east.

Johnny was alone, a prisoner of Little Wolf and the agent.

Sid Walsh was building a terrific head of steam. His mouth was drawn out long and tight, jaw muscles working beneath the heavy black burnsides. Johnny braced himself, half expecting the other's fist across his face. But Walsh had better control than that. He hung his thumbs into the armholes of his waistcoat, and with a head shot forward glowered at the tall young Indian in front of him.

"So!" He seemed to have difficulty speaking coherently. "We got us a troublemaker, have we? Thinks he can come in here and stir things up, sticking his nose in where he ain't concerned?"

Johnny Logan met his look squarely. "Those are my people out there. It has to concern me when I see them being cheated."

"They're a lazy, worthless pack of scoundrels! They choose to live like dogs—they deserve to be treated as such."

"They're what men like you have made them," Johnny retorted, fighting to keep his voice level. "Ten, fifteen years ago you'd have been scared to death of them. Now they're disarmed and helpless—and you know they don't dare to protest what's done to them, all you have to do is call the Army in." He shook his head. "No wonder there's nothing out there but hopelessness and defeat. I couldn't understand it at first. Having seen you, I understand it now!"

The other's eyes had narrowed, his thin lips pursed. He looked at Little Wolf who had stood impassively by during this, apparently not at all interested. Walsh said crisply, "I want this man put off the Reservation—and I don't want him coming back. See to it."

Little Wolf didn't need his orders spelled out. He nodded.

Johnny Logan rode away from the agency bracketed by a policeman at either stirrup. He was given no further chance to talk to anyone, and as they crossed the compound he got only curious glances. Over at the warehouse, distribution of rations proceeded. Johnny and his escort headed south, and very shortly the agency buildings dropped away from sight.

At first he made a few attempts at communication but his guards ignored him as though he wasn't there, and he gave up. They rode without hurry, no one speaking except when Little Wolf or the other policeman, whose name appeared to be Strong Runner, passed some remark in the Cheyenne tongue Johnny was unable to understand. Both men appeared in high good humor. After a while they began to pass jokes that set them slapping their thighs and whooping with laughter, and suddenly it was too much for Johnny Logan.

"Doesn't it mean anything to you," he burst out angrily, "that your own people are being starved and mistreated? While you stand by and do nothing!"

At his outburst their dark features closed down; they exchanged a look past their prisoner, and Strong Runner grunted something.

"Talk English!" Johnny snapped. "I heard you both talking it easy enough with your boss a while ago. Neither of you look very hungry," he went on, made reckless by his anger. "Looks to me like you've sold out yourselves to do Sid Walsh's dirty work! I'd think a man would have more pride than that."

The way Little Wolf's eyes blazed, Johnny expected the man to hit him or pull the revolver from his holster. But then a thin smile touched his lips. "Can a man eat pride?" he retorted scornfully. "The Indian's road goes downhill. The white agent gave me this"—he touched the metal badge pinned to his shirt—"and its medicine is strong. There is more power in it than in all the chiefs of the tribe who are no longer leaders of anything. I go this road!" And Strong Runner muttered in agreement.

"And I suppose you think that's being smart?" Johnny Logan said. "You were there in Walsh's office—you know how things are going. He's already in trouble with the Army for mishandling his job. If he loses the agency, what becomes of *you?*"

Little Wolf merely shrugged complacently. Strong Runner said, "Walsh plenty smart man, you bet. Too smart for Army!" And Johnny Logan gave up arguing—it was all too clear that these renegades had made their choice; purchased by special favors, and by the power and authority of the badges they wore, they'd let themselves be converted into tools of Agent Walsh. They would follow any order he gave them, whatever the consequences to their own people. . . .

They bore south through the rolling, lightly timbered hills, following no trail and meeting no one—all the living things they saw were a pair of does and their fawns that went drifting across a ridge and some quail they flushed out of a thicket of scrub pine and brush. Johnny began to wonder if this particular route had been chosen because the section of the Reservation it crossed was one where they weren't apt to be seen or perhaps raise questions.

Presently, coming out of timber at the head of a long slant, Little Wolf checked Johnny's horse by reaching for its bridle. He pointed past the head of Strong Runner's ewe-necked pony, off down the hill. "Just so you know," he said gruffly, "that creek is the Reservation boundary. You cross that—and you not come back."

Johnny Logan turned his head to follow the direction of the point. He saw the sweep of sun-browned grass, the boulder-strewn course of the stream at its bottom—a mere trickle lined by tules and willow. And then he took Strong Runner's fist, driven hard into his face, and the unexpectedness of it stunned and knocked him into Little Wolf. Before he could catch and right himself, a hand caught his shoulder and jerked him farther off balance, and Little Wolf hit him in turn. Stars streaked his vision and then the saddle went from under him and he was taking the long drop to the ground, too dazed to do anything about breaking his fall.

He landed hard, his head ringing, and trying to get some of his wind back when the other two, dismounted, hooked a hand under either arm and hauled him to his feet. They propped him on his boots and Little Wolf's harsh voice came through the dullness in his head; "We help you decide not to come back!" And they went to work.

They must have had expert training in the way to punish a prisoner, for they punished Johnny now. At first he tried gamely to fight back, but he was already dazed and the odds were against him. He managed to sting a grunt of pain from one of his enemies—he never knew which—when he got over a wild swing and felt his knuckles bounce off a hard cheekbone. But then he was down, and they let him stay there while they used their boots—heavy, white man's cowhides.

He never quite went under, though he half-consciously wished he could. At last it ended; everything went still and he lay there, too dazed to move—aware of his enemies standing over him, and the horses stomping restlessly as the smell of blood made them uneasy.

"You hear me?" Little Wolf's harsh voice came through to him. "Unless you want more—I think you not be back! Understand?"

Johnny Logan made no move, and no answer. Little Wolf gave an order to his companion, in the Cheyenne tongue; Johnny felt himself being lifted, and slung belly-down across a saddle. The jar of it did something to aggravate the damage he'd taken from their boots. The world went black.

CHAPTER V

Actually, it couldn't have been for very long. He found he was aware of an unpleasant swaying motion, of the earth sliding by somewhere below his head and beyond the reach of his dangling arms, of the black's muscled foreleg as it moved in and out of his vision. Then there was the sound and damp smell of running water, rippling shallowly among rounded stones. For the moment the swaying had ceased; the black was standing motionless—drinking, probably, from this stream that was the Reservation boundary.

Johnny Logan was able to figure as much, despite his dulled thinking process, and the pain that seemed to reach throughout his body without any definite center or location. Then abruptly there was an angry shout from Little Wolf; leather slapped sharply against hide and the black leaped forward as it took a lashing, evidently meant to drive it on. Stones rattled under steel shoes, shallow water splashed Johnny's face. After that he sensed that the horse had carried him across and was climbing the farther slope, in lunging strides that jarred pain through him again and sent consciousness slipping.

The throb of blood in his head helped drag him back to awareness. Somehow he understood that, having delivered him to the edge of the Reservation and administered a beating in warning not to return, the two members of the Indian police had no more interest in him, and he was alone. The black, without anyone to lead or goad it, had halted at last—probably having topped the ridge south of the boundary creek— and settled to feeding. Leaf shade flecked the ground, from trees rising about them. There was stillness except for the sound of the black's strong teeth tearing at the grass, and somewhere a jay scolding.

Extreme discomfort drove Johnny Logan, presently, to the effort of getting free of his jackknife position across the saddle; but his belt had been hooked over the horn, to anchor him, and at the moment he lacked the strength to work it loose. His struggles had no effect except to weaken him more . . . and then, surprisingly, someone was there to help him, someone with strong hands and a concerned if dimly-heard voice. A tug at his belt released it from the horn, let him slide free. When he felt the earth under his boots his knees buckled and he went down, falling against his horse which sidled away; he would have dropped on his face except for the hands that caught his shoulders, and lowered him gently down onto grass and soft pine needles.

Half conscious, he was aware of someone removing the neckcloth from about his throat.

Footsteps hurried away, almost silent in moccasins, while he lay battling weakness. Sometime later—it could have been only a moment or two, but time was without meaning—his benefactor had returned; the cloth that had been rung out in cold spring water was laid against his face. Though it burned like fire in the cuts, its touch revived him. The hand that held the cloth was gentle; and now, the voice spoke again, in the Cheyenne tongue that he failed to understand.

With an effort Johnny Logan got his eyes open, and blinked at the face he saw above him.

It was a round face framed by braids as black as night, with enormous dark eyes under level brows that were puckered now in concern. The girl's skin was a shade lighter than his own; her mouth looked soft, the lower lip full as a ripe berry.

When he didn't answer she spoke again—in English, this time: "Are you bad hurt?"

"Don't think I know yet," he said. The muscles of his jaw ached when he tried to talk; his bruised face felt like a stiff mask. "I took kind of a working over."

Her eyes flashed. "I saw them. Little Wolf and Strong Runner—they are bad men!"

"But they're good with their fists," he muttered. "And their boots!" Moved by anger, he tried to push himself to a sitting position. It was an ill-advised attempt; Johnny Logan fell back

72

gasping at the pain that stabbed through him.

The girl lifted a hand. "Oh! Be careful!"

"I guess I'd better!" he grunted. He laid an exploring hand to his side, and winced. "Feels like they might have done something to a rib." But he managed, with caution, to work his way up onto an elbow. Seeing he was determined, the girl helped him and then settled back on her haunches to look at him, as she anxiously worried that ripe lower lip.

"Thanks for your help," he said gruffly.

For all the dull, persistent gnaw of agony inside him, he couldn't help but notice the picture she made, kneeling there in a doeskin dress that was fringed and decorated with a pattern of porcupine quills. She had a nicely rounded bosom, a narrow waist, sturdy thighs; her arms, bare to the shoulders, looked brown and firm.

Johnny Logan asked, "How did you come to be here?"

"It was an accident. I was riding, and happened to notice the three of you together. I could see you were a stranger; it made me wonder what mischief Sid Walsh's police were up to, this time." Her mouth tightened. "It almost looked as though they tried to *kill* you!"

"Just teach me a lesson, was all." Gingerly he touched a knuckle to the sore places on his face. "I hope you didn't let either of them see *you!*"

She shook her head quickly. "I knew better

73

than that. . . . I watched while they put you on your horse and drove it across the boundary. I kept out of sight till I made sure they were gone."

Johnny frowned as he thought this over. His mind was still fuzzy, but aware enough for him to be bothered that she might have risked harm by interfering. She was not a large girl, he saw now; an Indian of course, like himself, and perhaps a year or two younger. She seemed to Johnny finely made. Her throat was delicate but the shoulders within the simple doeskin garment looked sturdy. The hands that had helped him down from his horse had been strong and sure.

"Well, anyway—thanks," he said again. "I—" It was difficult to get out words, since his throat and lips felt hot and parched. She must have realized that he was burning with thirst; she left him and a moment later was back again, from the spring or whatever water source where she had soaked the neckcloth.

She had had no way to carry water except in Johnny's own hat—he had lost it back yonder when he took his beating, but she must have picked it up and brought it along; he drank gratefully, spilling a good deal down the front of his shirt, and came up gasping and nodding to indicate he'd had enough. "That tasted great," he said. "I feel almost human." And to prove it he undertook to get to his feet.

The girl protested. "If you've got a broken rib—"

"I'm fine," he insisted.

Actually, a man's pride didn't like him to appear helpless in front of a young and healthy girl, and it was vanity rather than good sense that motivated him. It got him to his hands and knees and then, with an effort, clear to his feet, before the hurt inside all but clubbed him down again. Trees and grass and sky seemed to reel; he staggered and heard the girl exclaim, "I *knew* you shouldn't!" A brown arm went around his waist; her shoulder was there for him to lean on.

"Just give me a minute," he said doggedly. But things didn't seem to get any better.

In his ear the girl's voice said, "If we can get you onto your saddle, do you think you can hold on?"

"Of course," he said angrily. "I told you I'm fine!"

He got a hand on the horn and even managed the stirrup by himself, the black standing patiently; but without the girl to help, he never would have got his leg up and over and his weight placed in the saddle. She settled his right boot in its stirrup and then, looking anxiously up at him, said again, "You're sure you can stay there?"

Her own horse was a little pinto mare, that she rode bareback, with a rope halter and a single rein. She had the black's leathers and Johnny needed to do no more than keep his hands clamped on the horn and let her lead where she would. Even so, it seemed he could feel every step the black made; the effort of keeping himself upright took so much from him that he became almost indifferent to where the girl might be taking him—it was enough that, somewhere in his dulled brain, there was the assurance he could trust her.

They splashed through shallow water and over rounded stones, that clashed together musically under the horses' hoofs; it wasn't until they were climbing a rise beyond, that it came through to Johnny that what they had done was recross the boundary creek—she was leading him deliberately back onto the Reservation. This roused him to call a protest, and she turned back. "Where are we going?" he demanded.

"A place where you can get the attention you need." He waited for more, until he realized that was all she meant to say.

"But you don't understand!" he exclaimed. "I had some trouble with Walsh and he ordered me off the Reservation. What those two did to me was a warning not to come back. What would happen to you if they caught us?"

"They won't," she assured him, and with no further argument took the lead again. After that he knew vaguely that she was keeping an eye on him, making certain he stayed on his horse's back, but she didn't give him another chance to argue with her. . . .

Time became confused. The movement of the horse under him might have been over a tread-mill, for all Johnny Logan could be certain, but presently they were riding in toward a cluster of log buildings, and the horses came to a stand. He was aware of voices—one of them a man's deep tones, that issued from the heaviest and blackest beard he could ever remember seeing. There was a woman, too—white, like the man, with blue eyes and graying hair. Somehow she reminded him of Sarah Logan, his foster mother; for a moment he had a confused notion he was back home, at Star Ranch in the Bitterroots.

He was lifted from the saddle, and he cried out once and that was all he knew.

The room they put him in was pleasant and com-fortably furnished, if simple to an extreme—the bed where he lay was slung with ropes, the mat-tress filled with sweet-smelling hay. For other furnishings, there was only a small bedside table with a lamp on it, a chest of drawers, a single wooden chair. One corner of the room had been curtained off to make a closet. But there were embroidered runners on the table and the chest of drawers, a rag on the floor, fresh curtains at the window that gave him a pleasant view of grassy bottoms shining in the sun, and rolling, timbered hills.

It was a couple by the name of Cummings who lived here; Howard Cummings shooed his wife and the Indian girl from the room and set to work examining the strange youth's hurts. Despite his pirate's beard and growling voice he was a gentle man, with faded and bookish eyes behind octagonal spectacles—it seemed he had been sent here by an Eastern church group, to maintain and teach a school for the children of the Reservation Cheyenne. He told Johnny that, aside from Sid Walsh and the latter's waspish clerk, he and Mrs. Cummings were the only white residents at Walker Springs Agency.

"I've not always been able to keep on good terms with Walsh," he admitted, as he applied court plaster to a cut on Johnny Logan's forehead. "I think he resents my being here—the fact that I'm not under his authority. He hasn't much use for the school. To him, the Cheyenne children are bodies that have to be fed and clothed after a fashion, not minds that must be reached."

Johnny, scarcely able to breathe with the tight swath of bandage that had been wrapped about his body, said shortly, "The man's a crook and a grafter! He doesn't want anyone checking up on the way he runs his agency, and mistreats these people. It's because I dared to open my mouth, that I got beaten and thrown off the Reservation."

Cummings sighed deeply. "I've seen a great deal that's gone on here. I've done what I could, but it hasn't been much. Had I spoken up too loudly, Walsh could probably have pulled strings and got me expelled from the Reservation. Perhaps even—"

He didn't finish; Johnny Logan wondered at what he might have left unsaid. That he had been physically afraid, if not for himself then for the safety of his wife? In this isolated corner of Montana, any accident could happen—if nothing else, a fire of unexplained origin, destroying this couple's home and the school and all their possessions.

"Now that the military knows the sort of thing Walsh has been up to," Howard Cummings said, "surely they can put a stop to some of it." As though the talk had taken directions he didn't like, he ended it abruptly—slapping his knees and swinging to his feet from the chair beside the bed. Collecting the bandages and other materials, he told Johnny, "I doubt if that rib is actually broken; we'll keep it bound tight and see how it looks in the morning. Meanwhile I imagine you're getting hungry about now." He cocked a questioning eyebrow.

Johnny Logan hesitated, realizing how many hours had passed since his breakfast of trail rations. "I could eat," he admitted. "But I've been enough of a bother. Even putting you and Mrs. Cummings out of your bedroom . . ."

He didn't quite know how to read the look the other gave him. "But this isn't *our* room," Cummings said. "And don't worry about the food—Ellie loves to cook. I imagine she still has some of the stew left over from last evening. I'll have her put it on the stove."

Johnny was relieved at least to know there was a spare room—it made him feel less like an intruder; yet, oddly, there was something about the room that had a lived-in atmosphere. He was wondering about this when the quiet, and the sense of well-being after having his hurts tended to, dropped a soporific blanket over his thoughts and he felt himself drifting off to sleep.

It was a tantalizing smell of food that reached him and brought him awake again, a little later. On opening his eyes, the first thing he saw was the tray on the table beside him, holding a steaming cup of coffee and a plate of meat-and-vegetable stew. And then an awareness of someone else in the room raised his head, and he saw the girl sitting quietly on the chair, solemnly watching him.

As soon as his eyes touched her, her own warmed quickly in a smile. "You looked so comfortable, Johnny," she said, "I was about to take the tray back to the kitchen. It seemed wrong to wake you, and let you start hurting again."

"I don't hurt much," he said—and realized

it was true, so long as he stayed quiet. "And I realized I'm hungrier than I hurt. I'd hated to have missed this."

"Ella Cummings is a fine cook. Here—let me help." He started to protest, but he really did need someone to arrange his pillow and then ease him to a sitting position; he tried to keep the sharp twinge of pain from showing in his face, but was sure she saw it though he was grateful that she made no comment. She set the tray in his lap. "Can you manage now?"

"I can at least feed myself, if that's what you mean." He smiled and then sobered. "I haven't really thanked you for everything—and for bringing me here."

Her earnest mood quickly matched his own. "But you *did* thank me, Johnny Logan," she told him. "And now you'd better eat before that gets cold."

He nodded and set to work, while she sat and watched. In addition to the stew, there were biscuits and honey; he hadn't realized how hungry he was. But after a moment he paused to say, "I guess you learned my name from Mr. Cummings. I still don't know yours."

"My Indian name is Crow Wing," she told him. "But the Cummingses call me Anne. I've been with them so long, it seems natural."

"You *live* here?" Johnny exclaimed. "I didn't know."

"I've been without my parents, nearly ten years now. I was raised in the lodge of my father's brother, who has a large family of his own. Three years ago, when Mr. and Mrs. Cummings came to the Reservation, they took a liking to me and invited me to stay with them. They have been very good to me. I work hard at my studies, and help as I can with the children. . . ."

He nodded, understanding now. Her English came almost as naturally to her, as it did to him who had never spoken any other language— though he had noticed something in her speech that struck him as rather quaintly proper: That was probably because she had learned from a schoolmaster and his wife. On the other hand, he was glad they had not tried to make her over in the image of a white girl. She was pure Indian— from her moccasins and fringed doeskin dress, drawn in at the waist with a cord of rawhide, to the long braids, that were as softly black and lustrous as the crow's wing for which she was named. On the other hand, in some way that other, white girl's name seemed to suit her, too; he liked the simple sound of it: *Anne. . . .*

And then it struck him, and he almost dropped his fork. "For Pete's sake! It must be *your* room I've taken!" With a white girl, he thought, he wouldn't have been left in doubt: There would have been flounces on the bedspread, perhaps pictures on the wall cut from *Godey's Lady's*

Book. But being Indian as she was, Crow Wing—Anne—would likely never have thought of such things. "Well," he promised hurriedly, "I'll be out of here as soon as I finish eating."

"Don't be silly," she answered, a smile tugging at the corners of her mouth. "You know very well Mr. Cummings will never let you leave until you've had a night's rest. And don't fret about me—I don't mind being put out." She abruptly changed the subject. "Johnny Logan, it's your turn to tell me something about yourself. What is *your* Indian name?"

He hesitated, looking down at his plate. "I've never heard it," he said finally. "I was too little ever to remember my family." And he went on to tell her what he could—about the massacre, and about the rancher who saved his life and raised him as his own son.

"You see, you and I have quite a lot in common," he pointed out, "both being adopted by white families. Only you've stayed Cheyenne, while with me it happened so long ago that the Indian in me has been completely swamped. Inside, I feel I'm a white man—Matt Logan's son. I've never known any other life. And yet, most whites I've known have never let me forget, for a minute, that I'm pure-blood Cheyenne. What it comes down to, I don't really belong anywhere!"

The girl was frowning in sympathy. "Is that

why you came to the Reservation?" she suggested. "Looking for a place where you do belong?"

"Matt Logan died this spring," he explained. "And right away, I could see a rivalry beginning with his real son—my foster brother. I never wanted that. I had no claim to any part of the ranch. I decided it would be better, all around, if I struck out on my own. And, there was something else . . ." He reached for his shirt, that Cummings had laid aside on the bed while he bandaged Johnny's hurts. He dug out the medicine pouch that had been Matt Logan's dying gift to him; as the girl took it from his hand and wordlessly examined it, Johnny told her the story of the massacre on Cabinet Creek, of the brave who had died protecting a wounded child in his arms—and of the blind trail he had been following, with nothing more than the tiny painting of a bear for a clue.

"I talked to an old Indian at a trading post yesterday," he finished, "who believed the bag—or at least the painting—could have been made by a man he knew once, named Lame Elk. . . ."

He broke off as he saw the look in the girl's dark eyes. Anne said, "I know Lame Elk."

"You *know* him?" Johnny stared. "The same man? You're sure? Stands Talking, who told me about him, said he would have been dead long ago. He said there was barely a chance of my finding anyone on the Reservation who would even still remember him."

At that, she smiled a little. "Everybody knows that Stands Talking is a little crazy—he's lived by himself too long. No, I'm sure it's the same. The Lame Elk I know was once upon a time a great artist and craftsman. Of course, he is very, very old now."

Johnny Logan was having some trouble with his breathing. "According to Stands Talking, he would have to be if he's still alive! Can you tell me where to find him?"

"I'll do even better. Tomorrow I'll take you to see him." She hesitated. "I should warn you, though: Sometimes his mind seems far away. You never know for sure how it will be, with him."

"Does he have a family?"

"His third wife, who keeps his lodge for him. She's years younger, but it could be worth your while talking to her—she just might remember names and happenings Lame Elk has mentioned, from the past."

Johnny Logan, his limbs tingling with the excitement of what she had told him, demanded quickly, "Maybe we can go now?"

"Now?" she repeated, with a smile and shake of the head as she handed back the pouch. "I don't think Mr. Cummings would hear of that. In the morning, if you're feeling up to making the ride—"

Anne broke off. She must have seen him stiffen, read the sudden alarm in Johnny's face as he looked past her toward the window. She turned her head quickly, and he heard her gasp.

Three horsemen were coming across the sun-browned grass, directly toward the cluster of log buildings. "That looks like Walsh!" she cried. "And Little Wolf, and Strong Runner!" She leaped up from her chair and went to the window for a better look. "It is! And coming this way. I think they're following our tracks. . . . Oh, Johnny! What do you suppose—?"

Whirling from the window, she cried out as she saw Johnny out of bed and stooping over his saddlebags, working at the pocket fastenings. "What are you doing?" she exclaimed.

She fell silent, dark eyes wide in alarm, as he straightened with one hand pressed against the pain of his damaged rib, and the other holding a Colt revolver.

CHAPTER VI

A half hour after his callers left the agency office, Sid Walsh was still slumped motionless in his chair, still in a towering temper and in no mood to do any work. When Beaver Tail opened the screen and came in, Walsh gave the Indian a baleful glare. "What do *you* want?" he snapped; and then, as the man offered a folded piece of paper, "Where'd you get that?"

"Sergeant left it, said give to you."

"Well, you certainly took your damn sweet time!" Scolding had no effect at all on the man. With a shrug Walsh took the note, opened it and read the scrawled and nearly illiterate writing. Slowly his face suffused with color; he swore, and crumpled the paper in his fist. "Damn it, if you'd only given this to me a half hour ago—" But the blank imperturbability of that flat Cheyenne face again made anger futile. Walsh gave it up with a shake of the head, and a wave of the hand to dismiss him. Then, as an afterthought, he ordered, "Saddle my horse. Just try not to take all day!"

Beaver Tail, with features as expressionless as a board, merely looked at him and then, quite deliberately, turned his back and stalked out, leaving Walsh glowering after him. You couldn't touch an Indian, or get behind that dead mask he showed you—you could not do a damn thing to any of them. That was the reason he hated them; if he held them in contempt, it was because a man was bound to despise those who docilely permitted him to exploit them.

Walsh rose, went back into his living quarters to strap on his spurs and get his hat and corduroy jacket. A precaution sent him to his desk again, where he opened a drawer and took out the cedar-handled six-shooter that he kept there, with its cartridge-studded belt wrapped around it. He slung the belt about his lean waist and fastened it, settled the holster comfortably. Walsh was in no sense a gunman, but three men at various times had gone down before that gun, two of them permanently.

He was waiting before the office, pacing the gravel with shortening patience as the flag snapped overhead at the top of its pole, when Beaver Tail finally brought his horse—a Roman-nosed brown whose flanks bore the spur marks from Walsh's impatient handling. He snatched the reins from the Indian, took a moment to check the cinch, then stepped to the saddle. The spurs sank deep and gravel spurted at the animal's lunge forward. Walsh cursed the animal under his breath, and swung it in the southward direction Little Wolf and Strong Runner had taken when they rode off with their prisoner.

Thanks to the delay in receiving the message

left for him by Ed Bailey, he knew the chances were slim of overtaking them. Still, he had to make the effort. He pushed the horse hard, taking out his anger with the spurs, and got it up to a gallop and held it there, unrelenting. The ground blurred by and he watched the shifting horizons with eyes slitted against the wind of his own travel. And though he had no reason to be surprised, chagrin made him curse savagely when he finally sighted his two policemen returning at an easy pace—alone.

They showed him that same damnable impassivity, their dark faces incurious and unmoved, as he pulled rein. With the winded horse straining and trembling between his knees, Sid Walsh demanded harshly, "Where is he?"

"You say throw him off Reservation," Little Wolf reminded him. "We do that."

Walsh drew a breath to settle his poorly controlled temper. "There's a change," he said roughly. "I want him back. We'll have to go after him." He didn't miss their deliberate exchange of looks, whose amusement and contempt for such unexplainable contradictions couldn't have been clearer. Stung, he shouted at them: "All right—all right! Something's come up. Anyway, it's none of your damned business! You do what you're told . . . or I'll take those badges off your shirts, and find myself somebody else who knows how to take orders."

That threat shook them, as it never failed to do—it was his ultimate hold over them. Having once worn the badge of the Indian police, none of these simple savages wanted to be stripped of such power and prestige and extra advantages as it gave them. He didn't need to say any more; he simply kicked the brown horse forward, and the two Cheyenne made way for him and then fell in, silently, at either flank. In silence they rode, retracing the route they'd just covered. Walsh set a stiff pace, spurred by the need to prevent the man called Johnny Logan escaping from him.

They came to the steep-sided trough, and the rocky trickle of water that was the Reservation's boundary. They swept down the bank and halted briefly while Sid Walsh demanded, "Which way from here?"

A gesture of Little Wolf's arm pointed ahead, up the farther rise. But as the white man lifted the reins again the Cheyenne said, "He maybe not ride far."

Walsh gave him a sharp look. "No? Why not?"

"Before we let him go, we beat him up some. He don't feel so good. We have to put him across his saddle."

The white man let out his breath. "Well, now, why the hell couldn't you have told me this earlier?" he said. "It could mean we've got a chance, after all! He may be lying on the prairie somewhere, right now—just waiting for us to come and pick him up!" Impatiently he kicked his horse across the stream and climbed the lift of the hill beyond, that was crowded by a patchy stand of timber. But a look at the sweep of empty range beyond disappointed him. There was no man down there, and no horse either. It wasn't going to be that easy.

Then Strong Runner called for him to wait.

As Walsh turned impatiently, anxious to be gone, he saw Strong Runner had halted and was staring at the ground. "What now?" Walsh demanded. The Indian stabbed a pointing finger; he looked and saw nothing, and said irritably, "Hell! Whatever you make out, there, it don't say anything to *me.*"

So Strong Runner explained, with patience that Walsh suspected was touched with scorn for the white man's blindness: "Tracks. Other rider meet him here. Second horse not shod—Indian pony."

"From the Reservation?" Walsh snapped him up. Strong Runner, still reading the sign that seemed perfectly clear to him, nodded as he pointed back down the slope, though at a different angle from the one they had ridden.

"Rider come up there," he said. Now he lifted a leg across his pony's back, slid easily to the ground; there he paced about, careful where he stepped, his whole attention focused.

"Moccasins," he pointed out. Walsh, scowling, leaned from the saddle but still saw nothing in the pine litter covering the ground beneath the trees. "They both get off their horses. One *fall* down . . ." The way he said it, there could hardly be any doubt which one that would have been— after all, if this pair gave Johnny Logan a beating, it could be assumed they had done the job right and really punished him. Strong Runner pointed to the horse droppings—even Walsh could see those, and smell them too. "They not stay very long."

"All right, all right! Where did they *go?*" Walsh demanded irritably.

Little Wolf, also dismounted, had already worked that out. "This way," he said, pointing. Walsh stared.

"Right back onto the Reservation?" he exclaimed, incredulous. His jaw set hard. "If so, then it's the stupidest mistake that Logan fellow ever made!" A clipped order sent his Indians leaping onto their horses, and they went pouring back down the hill toward the place where the two riders had recrossed the boundary stream.

On the other side, they overshot their mark and lost the trail for a while in a fan of rocky gullies, and in hunting it used up valuable time that had Walsh fuming with thwarted impatience. But he kept his men at the search and presently they picked up the tracks once more. The sun was dragging down toward the western hills, warning that if they weren't careful dusk would catch them; still, even trackers as good as these had to take their time, and proceed with caution. Walsh held a curb on his temper, and as time dragged out and he saw the course the trail was leading them, he began to feel that he knew where it would end up. He was positive, some time before they actually brought the school and the house of the schoolmaster into sight.

Suspicions and dislike rankled as they rode in toward the buildings. That fellow Cummings— and his wife, too—had been a problem and an inconvenience for Walsh ever since their arrival at the Reservation. Having another white man around, independent of the agency and openly sympathetic to these damned Indians, had hampered his style and made him miss a number of opportunities for turning a good profit—and in fact, he wasn't sure but what Cummings might have had something to do with the military moving in and taking matters of supply entirely out of his hands.

If there'd been any real proof of it, he'd never let it go without finding some way to even the score.

Right now, Walsh had a careful eye on the one-roomed log school building. He knew what went on in there, and he hated it—Cummings and his wife working on those Indian kids, teaching them to speak and read English and filling them full of troublesome notions which they passed on to their elders; left in ignorance and savage superstition, the Cheyenne were much more tractable and uninclined to question his control of their lives. This being ration day, there were no classes. The silent and seemingly empty building made a very likely place for someone to hole up while recovering from a beating. *If he's hiding there,* Walsh told himself, *whether or not with Cummings' O.K.—I've got my excuse to burn the goddam thing down on top of him!*

But the tracks apparently didn't point that way. His scouts led him, instead, straight to the door of Cummings' living quarters, and as they came up the door opened and the schoolteacher, himself—with his big frame that would have looked more fitting on a blacksmith—stepped outside. Mild blue eyes peered at Walsh through the flashing lenses; his deep voice rumbled: "Something I can do for you?"

Walsh was in no mood to mince matters. "I'm looking for the pair of Indians that rode in here, it wouldn't have been much more than an hour ago. Where are they?"

The other showed him no expression whatever. He said, "What do you want with them?"

"Then you admit they're here?"

"I didn't say that."

"What I want," Walsh said, his voice rising as he began to lose hold of his temper, "is my own personal business! Will you turn them over—or do you want trouble with me?"

Cummings refused to match his anger. Calmly he said, "I did see two Indians. I don't pretend to know every Cheyenne on the Reservation, but they could have been the ones you're talking about. One looked as though he had taken a bad beating—he could hardly stay on his horse. They wouldn't say what had happened to him. . . ."

Walsh broke in, impatiently. "All right, all right! What *did* they say?"

"The other man was belligerent. He wanted whiskey—said his friend needed it. I think he may have been a little drunk himself. Naturally I told him he'd come to the wrong place for that. I offered to do what I could for his hurt friend, but he wouldn't let me. He got to talking loud and finally he brought out a gun."

"A gun?" Sid Walsh snapped.

"It was a revolver of some sort—the kind, I think, people out here call a 'hogleg.' He began trying to bully me into giving him extra shells for it, but I guessed from that that the gun was empty and I told them both to leave. After a while they did. That's all I know."

Walsh, considering this story, demanded, "Which way did they ride?"

Cummings pointed north and east. "Past that big pine you see on the ridge. I watched until they were out of sight, because I wasn't sure the hurt one would make it. His friend had to lead his horse by the reins. . . ."

The command that Walsh gave his men was unneeded. Little Wolf had already started sorting out the confusion of hoof marks, in trampled dirt before the doorway. He rode on for a few yards, then suddenly looked around and lifted a hand to signal that he had found tracks of departing horses. Sid Walsh picked up the reins, impatient to be gone, but he took long enough to give the schoolteacher a close look. "I thought for a minute you were going to give me trouble," he said gruffly. "I'm glad you've got sense enough not to. I run this agency; you teach your school, and don't interfere, and we can get along. But the first time I catch you meddling in my affairs— you're finished!"

It was a warning he had given before—one he thought bore repeating, on occasion, to keep the pious fool in his place. Cummings made no answer at all, merely looked at him with those mild blue eyes in that bearded, craggy face that sometimes seemed utterly guileless but, at others, almost like a clever mask.

Walsh had no more time to waste here. Ed Bailey's message was still goading him. That troublemaker who called himself Johnny Logan had still to be captured, as well as his friend with the revolver that might or might not have shells in it. The day was getting short, the trail colder.

He settled his boots into the stirrups, and kicked the brown with the spurs. With Little Wolf ranging ahead to read sign, the three of them rode across the grassy slope toward the ridge where a lone pine lifted into the lengthening gleam of afternoon sunlight.

Johnny Logan heard that scene—loud and angry voices, beyond the open window—as he leaned against the bedroom wall with his head spinning from that too-hasty scramble to reach his gun. The gun was in his fist but the girl had his wrist trapped and her body was pressed against his, to keep him from making some rash movement that would be heard by his enemies outside. While they listened, he read the anxiety in those eyes so close to his own, heard her shallow breathing and almost thought he could feel the swift beating of her heart.

And then the horses had started up again, moving past the window as their riders struck out on the false lead Howard Cummings had given them. The drum of hoofs quickly faded; staring at the girl, Johnny blurted the thought that startled him: *"Whose trail are they following?"*

The black eyes began to sparkle with amusement. "Mine," she said, and stepping back she grinned when she saw his look. But she sobered quickly as she explained: "We didn't *know* that anyone would try to follow us, but if they did the tracks were sure to lead them straight here—I couldn't take the time to lay a false trail, when you were having so much trouble simply staying in the saddle. But after we got you in the house, I took both horses and headed for some outcroppings I know about. It wasn't hard to lose the sign there, and double back."

"Where are the horses now?" he wanted to know.

"Quite close—but safe hidden. There's really nothing to worry about. Little Wolf and Strong Runner"—she spoke the names scornfully—"they think they're clever, because they wear shields on their shirtfronts and get to lord it over everybody; but really, they're very stupid men. And after the story we made up for Mr. Cummings to tell, I'm sure Sid Walsh must think the trail ends up at Piping Rock, or one of the other agencies."

Johnny nodded, remembering. "That Major Harriman said he was on his way to Piping Rock. Walsh may get the idea I intend to catch up with him there. . . ."

The sound of Cummings' solid tread preceded him as he came into the room. If he had been under any strain during the encounter with Walsh, he failed to show it. He said, "They're gone."

"You really handed them a whopper!" Johnny Logan said, and saw the other's genial nod.

"Didn't I though?" the schoolteacher agreed

98

placidly. "It just proves that an honest man can make a fool out of a crook, if he puts his mind to it." Frowning then, he added, "Why do you suppose the man is suddenly so anxious to get his hands on you?"

"I wish I knew," Johnny said bleakly. "Earlier, he was satisfied just to see me gone from the Reservation. Apparently something's happened, that made him change his mind."

Anne said, "But meanwhile, what are you going to do, Johnny?"

"Why, you promised me that tomorrow, we'd go visit Lame Elk."

"Yes, I know I promised." Her dark eyes clouded. "But, that was before—I mean, if they should manage to lay hands on you . . ." Quickly she shook her head. "Johnny, it's too dangerous now!"

"No! I came here for a purpose," he said firmly. "I've ridden a long way, and you can't expect me to give it up just on account of this. On a reservation the size of this one, it shouldn't be too hard to keep out of Sid Walsh's road."

Cummings had been watching them both and he said firmly, "I don't know what this quarrel is about, or who made what sort of promises. But I can tell you now, young man, you're not going anywhere until you've had a couple of good meals, and a night's rest. We'll keep you out of sight, just in case. By morning, if there's no sign that Walsh has caught on to the trick we played on him—and you look in good enough condition to ride—then, we'll see . . . ."

They had dinner in one end of the long main room that served as both sitting room and kitchen, eating on a table and chairs that looked as though Cummings himself might have hewn them with his big, capable hands. His wife was a small, birdlike woman, and an excellent cook; the roast she took from the wood-burning black oven was done to perfection, and it made Johnny think of the meals Sarah Logan had put together back at Star. He said so, and that led to questions about the ranch in the Bitterroots.

Anne, in particular, wanted to know about the black stud, which with the fall of dusk had been brought in and was feeding on hay and oats in Cummings' stable. "He's a beautiful animal. Where did you get him?"

"I helped Matt Logan catch him," Johnny said. "And I broke and trained him to cow work. He was pretty mean at first; one of the boys on the ranch named him 'Satan.' But with me he's a perfect gentleman—though I admit he doesn't like strangers much. When I left the ranch, he was the only thing I took with me."

"Don't you ever intend to go back?" Mrs. Cummings asked.

"Oh, I guess the latch string will always be out

for me at Star," Johnny answered. But he shook his head. "I doubt I'll ever go back to stay. Even though I was raised there, it's a white man's ranch—in a white man's country. More and more, growing up, I came to know I didn't really belong."

Howard Cummings, studying him with a shrewd eye, asked bluntly, "And is it your thought, that perhaps you belong here on the Reservation?"

He hesitated. "I guess that's something I'll have to find out, isn't it?"

Later, he stepped outside with his host to stand before the door, getting the smell and the size of the night with its glitter of stars across the sky. Cummings had fired up a briar pipe; its glow lighted his bearded face as he told Johnny about his work in the school that stood, dark and silent, a few rods away. Johnny said, into a silence, "There was a young fellow I met today at the agency, who seemed to take a dislike to me from the word go. And that's too bad, because I was very much impressed with him. I wonder if you know him. He called himself Swooping Hawk. . . ."

The bearded head moved in a nod; the white man's voice sounded heavy with regret when he answered: "Ah, yes. I know him well. He, and Anne, are the two brightest youngsters I've had come through the school. But I'm afraid that young fellow's mind was closed, from the start, to anything I tried to put into it.

"Swooping Hawk distrusts and hates everything to do with the white man. He wouldn't have anything to do with learning to read or write—but I put him at the same desk with Anne, and he is naturally intelligent enough that I think through her he learned quite a bit, in spite of himself. But in the end, he rebelled. He dropped out of school, and nothing I've been able to do or say could make him come back. Anne has tried, too, but even she failed."

Johnny was silent. The older man continued. "Frankly, I worry about him. What will become of a boy like that—with his quick mind, and no way to put it to use? He's absorbed all the culture of his people—a fine thing, but that's a dying way of life. And there's a bunch of the young bucks who look up to him and follow him in everything he does, because he's a natural leader—only, what he'd like to do is lead them into the past. Meanwhile he has nothing but hatred for Walsh and the agency police. If something can't be done, I'm afraid he's headed for serious trouble—and it bothers me very, very much. . . ."

A coyote sounded his lonely cry somewhere back in the hills. The schoolteacher sighed and knocked his pipe against a post, sparks streaming on the sage-scented night wind. Together they turned and re-entered the house.

CHAPTER VII

Johnny Logan won his argument about sleeping arrangements—he spent the night on a couch in the main room, so that Anne could have her bed. Come morning, he still knew well enough that he had taken a hard beating; when he awoke at first light, he had to bite back a groan as he rose and moved silently about, getting into his clothes. But as he began to limber up, the worst of his body's soreness began to be worked out.

The swellings on his face, caused by the fists of Little Wolf and Strong Runner, had gone down. Even the pain of the damaged rib was no more than he could handle.

His hosts, too, were early risers. The sun hadn't yet topped the hills when Howard Cummings came out to say good morning to Johnny and start shaking down the ashes and building a breakfast fire in the black wood range. Johnny fetched a bucket of well water and then went out to check on the horses in the shed. As the sky took on sunrise colors, he stood close against a corner of the shed and studied the surrounding open land, still thinking of Walsh and his agency police. But he could make out nothing he read as danger; relieved at this, he gave the animals feed and water, and promised the black they would be taking the trail again.

He was interested to see the school, and after breakfast Anne took a moment to show it to him. It was furnished and equipped barely and simply enough: a few long benches and trestle tables for the Indian kids, a desk and chair for Cummings, all obviously hand-hewn by the teacher himself. There were pictures of Lincoln and Washington, a flag on a standard in the corner, a pot-bellied heating stove in a box of cinders.

Anne opened a cupboard and showed Johnny the scant supply of slates and books—"We make do with what we have," she explained. "The Eastern people who pay Mr. Cummings to run the school can't afford much more than his wages. *I* don't ask any pay, of course, for what I'm able to do helping out." Her own job was to keep things tidy—and the schoolroom was spotless—as well as helping some of the youngsters with their lessons, and generally making herself useful in any way she could.

But she had been allowed to take today off, for the promised visit to Lame Elk's village. It was still early when they started out. The bad rib gave some trouble as Johnny was handling the heavy stock saddle, and afterward when he mounted up; but he kept any hint of pain from showing in his face. The tight bandage, and a reasonable amount of care, should let the damage mend itself in good time.

Their direction lay east and a little north; they

rode warily, always remembering the threat from Walsh's police. But Anne knew the country and she picked a course that kept them below the skyline; Johnny left this to her, and began to enjoy himself. It was a pleasant day, of warm sun and a cool and steady wind. It was the girl, though, who made this an occasion for Johnny Logan.

In her company, time and distance became nothing at all. From moment to moment he seemed to be learning new things about her, new facets of the personality that lay behind those smiling lips and liquid dark eyes. He almost forgot, for a time, the purpose of this ride—the eagerly anticipated meeting with Lame Elk that might end the quest that had brought him so far, hunting for his past.

Johnny Logan wondered if this could be what people meant, when they spoke about falling in love.

A little short of noon, they brought Lame Elk's village into view. Johnny felt his pulse quicken, and he wondered if some dim racial memory might be stirring in him as he looked upon a sight that he had so often imagined, but could not remember actually seeing with his own eyes.

It seemed a natural choice for an encampment—a well-grassed flat, with water and pine timber for firewood. The village itself struck him at first as an antigodlin scatter of tepees, pole ends bunched against the sky above their painted canvases, and a smudge of campfire smokes blown about by the wind; but as they drew nearer the place sorted itself into an orderly pattern, perhaps two dozen lodges arranged in a wide circle; beyond, on the open meadow, he could see a fair-sized herd of spotted Indian ponies feeding. Under the wide Montana sky, dotted with summer clouds, he knew his first view of Cheyenne village life was one he would never forget.

Communal sounds swelled to meet them; a busy babble of voices, the shouting of children, the barking of dogs. As they rode in, Johnny Logan found himself engrossed with everything he saw and heard—after all, if fate hadn't decreed otherwise, he himself would once have been one of these dark-skinned, half-naked youngsters that he could see tumbling about underfoot, in some mysterious game at whose rules he could only guess. All of this would have been second nature to him: this woman stirring something in a pot slung above a fire; yonder, the half-glimpsed interior of a painted canvas tepee, and someone moving about there; a young woman on her knees scraping a pegged-down deerskin, and glancing up to the infant in its cradleboard hanging above her head; an old man completely absorbed in something he seemed to be carving. . . .

A troubled question grew, unbidden: But where are all the *young* men?

106

He was about to say something to the girl about this when she veered away toward a tepee set somewhat apart from the others. It looked deserted—the tent flap drawn closed, no smoke rising—but as Anne slipped from her pony a woman came trudging from the direction of the stream-side timber bearing an axe and an arm-load of chopped kindling.

She was a big woman, shapeless in a cheap cotton dress, her braided hair streaked with gray. She returned Anne's greeting with an expression-less nod and then, still holding her burdens, listened as the girl spoke in their native tongue. Johnny, having also dismounted, could only stand helplessly by, unable to understand a word of what was being said. The woman gave him looks that he thought were filled with suspicion. She shook her head, said something that sounded to him like a curt refusal. There was more talk, and at last the girl turned back to Johnny.

"Something's wrong," he interpreted. "She won't let me see Lame Elk?" A worse thought struck him. "Or—has he died?"

She grinned at the disappointment in his face. "Nothing that bad, Johnny. He's just asleep, and his wife doesn't want to wake him—he's a very old man, you know. I'm afraid we'll just have to wait a little while. I hope you don't mind."

"Mind?" he said, and answered her smile. "Why should I mind? When I'd just convinced myself I'd come all this way for nothing!"

"We can look around the village, if you'd like."

"I would," Johnny Logan said.

They walked slowly, leading their horses. To the girl of course all this was very familiar; Johnny knew she was watching his face, studying his reactions with what he thought must be at least partly amusement. "Well," she said finally, a smile tugging at the corners of her full lips, "do you think you'd want to come and live in a Reservation village?"

He hesitated. "That's a big question," he answered seriously. "If you mean, would I like living in a tent after being brought up in a white man's house—I think I could get used to it."

"I've lived both ways," she reminded him. "When you can look up through the smoke-hole of your lodge and see the stars overhead, you feel you belong to nature. The walls of a white man's house shut nature out."

"On the other hand," Johnny argued, "who gets any closer to nature than a cowpuncher who spends his days in the saddle, and uses it for a pillow at night?" He hesitated, before raising the question that bothered him. "I've been wondering, though. All I seem to see here are women and children, and old men. The youngsters keep busy enough, and the women have plenty to do; and I guess an old man can always sit and gossip and soak up the sun. But what about the young men? Where are they? What does a fellow like Swooping Hawk find to do with his time?"

They had been talking earlier about Swooping Hawk, and what Cummings had said of him. Johnny suspected that Anne was worried about her friend; she said now: "It isn't easy for them. Always, it's been the job of the men in the prime of life to do the hunting, and protect the tribe from its enemies. . . ."

"But now that the Cheyenne has been beaten for good, and his food is doled out to him twice a month on ration day—?"

She seemed to reach a decision. "I want you to come with me," Anne said suddenly. "There's someone I'd like you to talk to. . . ."

The lodge she led him to had its canvas rolled up around the bottom, to allow circulation of air in the warm noontime. There was evidence of a woman's work, in a deerskin drying on a rack, and in the smoke from a cooking fire curling up from the smoke-hole, but she seemed to be elsewhere at the moment. As they approached a man stepped from the tepee's entrance.

He was a fine figure of a man, in his middle years, the flesh of his face weather-worn and fined down to a hawkish contour of wide brow and strong cheekbones and high-bridged nose. He was tall and fiercely erect, though his hair was streaked with gray; within the quilled and fringed shirt he looked deep-chested, flat-bellied. He greeted Anne warmly, and then deep-set eyes turned on the stranger as she spoke at some length in the language of the People.

She turned to her companion. "Johnny, this is Leads-His-Horse. He is Swooping Hawk's father. . . ."

A moment later Johnny found himself seated upon the ground before the lodge, facing the man and with Anne beside him. Leads-His-Horse spoke English with the stiffness of a proud nature, and the unfamiliarity of a language learned with difficulty in the later years of his life; but as with all the Cheyenne, his stumbling speech was more than compensated for by the eloquent gestures that went with it. Johnny Logan watched his hands, fascinated by the way they pointed up and underscored the inflection and meaning of every word he uttered.

He said, "You know my son. . . ."

"We met yesterday."

"And you look for word of your father." Abruptly the man held out a hand toward him, palm up. Johnny looked at Anne.

She explained quickly, "I told him about the medicine pouch, Johnny. He wants to see it."

Johnny Logan took it from his pocket. Leads-His-Horse turned the little bag over and over in his fingers, his dark face scowling in concentration. He looked for a long time at the faded paintings; Johnny heard him say the one word, "*nahgui*"—he knew that was the *tsis-tsis-tas* name for bear. The black eyes lifted from their inspection, then. To Johnny he said, in his halting English, "I think Lame Elk make this, maybe—long ago. But Lame Elk maybe not remember. Lame Elk old—old!—and sick in head." And then, as he handed the pouch back to Johnny, his face took on bitterness and he added: "Swooping Hawk *young,* and sick in head!"

Anne protested quickly, "That's not true!"

"He try to think the old times still here," Leads-His-Horse continued doggedly. "I tell him the old times are gone. The land—gone! Buffalo gone! Without buffalo, what is left of Cheyenne? Even our lodges now made from white-eyes' canvas." His mouth drew down in angry disgust. "Canvas no good! Canvas let in rain and cold; canvas wear out."

"Johnny," Anne put in quickly, "I wish you could have seen what it was like once! When I was little, our lodges were still made of buffalo hides. In the evening, with the fires inside, they glowed just like lanterns. You never saw anything more beautiful!"

"Buffalo all gone now," Leads-His-Horse said. "Times change. But Swooping Hawk not know this. Swooping Hawk not *want* to know." The fierce eyes raked Johnny Logan—his style of dress, his whole appearance. "But, I see *you* know."

"I can't take credit for that," Johnny Logan protested. "Or blame either, for deserting the Indian way. Anne must have told you, it was an accident. I had nothing to do with it."

The older man might not even have heard. "Swooping Hawk, and the other young braves, should learn from you."

"I'm afraid your son doesn't think there's anything I could teach him. In fact, he's got no use for me at all. He calls me a white Indian."

"He was born too late," Anne said. "It's terribly hard for the young men. When they were little, the Cheyenne was still free; they grew up on tales of the warpath and the hunts, and pony-stealing raids against the Crows. And now—all that is over. There is no glory left. Herded here on the Reservation, like cattle or horses, there's nothing for the young men to *do*. They spend their time in the hills, in make believe, trying to pretend the old days are still alive."

Johnny Logan didn't like to ask the next question. He was thinking about old Stands Talking as he said, "I was wondering, what about alcohol?"

A terrible light kindled in the other man's eyes. A fist raised, clenched. "Firewater is white man's worst weapon against the Indian!"

Anne put in quickly, "It has to be said for Walsh and the other agents, that they're at least keeping whiskey away from our young men. But after all, the Cheyenne have nothing to trade for it except their ponies and a few beaver pelts. Then, too, if liquor was allowed on the Reservation, someone like Walsh might not be able to keep control, and bend the People to his will with only a handful of agency police, the way he does now."

"Walsh!" Leads-His-Horse echoed the name bitterly. "He hates the Cheyenne! Always he cheats, he steals from us. And the People are helpless."

"Now the Army's watching him," Johnny said, "he'll surely have to watch his step at least."

The other man's shrug was eloquent enough. "A few moons ago, the white man's army wanted to kill all the Cheyenne. Now they save us from Sid Walsh?"

"All the Army wants," Howard Cummings had said last evening, "is that the Indians be kept quiet. As long as there's no active trouble on the reservations, they look the other way and let agents like Walsh run things to suit themselves. I can only hope the Indians won't finally be driven to desperate measures—and then the Army simply walk in and squash them flat!"

It was a depressing picture. Johnny found he had nothing at all to say.

The sounds of the village, breaking in upon their somber thoughts, seemed like the voice of a vanished way of life. Leads-His-Horse sighed and got to his feet, with a grace of movement that seemed still youthful despite his years. Johnny Logan thought he was going into the tepee, ending this meeting, but instead he picked up something that leaned against the canvas and turned with it in his hands and Johnny saw what it was—a steel-bladed hoe, a white man's tool, such as he remembered seeing yesterday at the agency warehouse. He stood awkwardly holding it and his face and his voice were heavy with bitterness.

"White man wants Indian to become farmer. But, Indian is proud—Indian stands straight before his enemies; Indian does not tear the flesh of his mother, the earth. That is work for squaws!" His chest swelled with a long breath. "But if the Cheyenne must now bend his back, and break the ground with a hoe for his food because the white man has said so—then, he must!"

Abruptly he tossed the hoe aside and, stooping, entered the tepee. Staring after him, Johnny Logan heard the girl explaining: "He and some of the other tribal leaders have been trying to set an example for the young men, by taking out land allotments and putting them into crops—just to show that farm work isn't below the dignity of a Cheyenne. It's a very hard thing—at their age, and after the kind of life they knew. And I'm afraid the young men don't show any signs of following their example. They just look on with contempt. . . ."

Johnny soberly nodded his understanding. Not because he had been born an Indian, but because he had been raised by a foster father who was a cattleman, he didn't have much patience himself with the idea of being tied to one tiny plot of ground. He had heard somewhere of one old Shoshoni chief who, when they tried to make a farmer of him, was supposed to have cried out in exasperation, "God damn a potato!" And how could you blame a man for that?

Leads-His-Horse had returned, and a moment later a woman came from the lodge bringing food—flat wooden bowls of some kind of venison stew, and chunks of fried bread. For the guests there were ugly, heavy Government-issue eating utensils which their host scorned, preferring to use his fingers in the customary way. Johnny ate eagerly, finding the food delicious.

As they were finishing, a Cheyenne lad came running up with word that jarred other matters from his mind. Anne interpreted for him: "Lame Elk has awakened. We're to go back to his tent now."

They thanked Leads-His-Horse for his hospitality, and for the talk, and Johnny felt a keen rise of anticipation as they made their way again through the camp. Sensing this, Anne spoke a warning: "Please don't expect too much, Johnny. I hope you're going to learn what you want; but as I told you yesterday—Well, maybe you'll see what I mean."

Lame Elk's squaw—Owl Woman, according to Anne—greeted them again at the entrance of the lodge. Without a word she pulled back the opening flap, and motioned them inside. Johnny Logan, who had never been inside a tepee, was struck by the amount of room it contained. There was no feeling of cramped space, and the glow of afternoon light through the canvas made it seem even larger—enclosed, and yet intimately connected with the natural world outside. Around the rim of the oval interior was all the room needed for storage bags, and for what Johnny supposed were mattresses, made of willow rods and rolled up and placed out of the way when not in use. Pots and baskets and clothing hung from the poles that formed the framework of the lodge. Smoke rose from the rectangular firepit, framed with stones, to the hole where the lodge poles met.

Huddled against a backrest, very near the firepit with its glowing bed of coals, sat the oldest man Johnny Logan thought he had ever laid eyes on.

Lame Elk's face seemed made of crumpled burnt leather that had fallen in upon the skull beneath—only a few straggles of lank white hair still clinging to the barren scalp, the lashless eyes turned milky, the toothless jaw afflicted by a constant wobble. Within his ancient buckskins, his bones must have been as thin and brittle as sticks. Looking at the painful, arthritic bundles that were his hands, Johnny wondered in some disbelief if those fingers could ever have achieved the perfect workmanship of the pouch he carried in his shirt.

Johnny took a long breath. He could see no indication that Lame Elk was even aware of visitors. Something made him lower his voice as he asked the girl, "Does he speak any English?"

"None at all," she said, in the same hushed tone. "We'll let Owl Woman talk to him."

The woman had entered the lodge behind them. Johnny, standing helplessly by, listened as she addressed her husband; he watched Lame Elk's face for any signs of comprehension, and with sinking emotions failed to see them. And he felt Anne's hand slip into his own, her fingers closing on his in a way that told him she knew his disappointment.

"Johnny, maybe if you showed him the pouch . . ."

He got it out, and going down on his knees he held it so that the faded paintings were directly before the old man's eyes. The voice of the squaw continued its steady drone, but nothing seemed to draw a response. When, after a moment, Owl Woman at last fell silent, Johnny didn't have to be told what it meant. Slowly he shook his head. "I guess it's no use at all."

A single drop of spittle formed and ran from a corner of the old man's slack lips.

With a sigh, Johnny Logan climbed back to his feet. He met the girl's unhappy look. "Oh, Johnny!" she said softly. "I *am* sorry! I tried to warn you not to hope too much. He's not always like this. Sometimes his mind seems to clear and you can talk to him. But then, again—"

"It's all right," he said, and managed to smile a little. "At that, I came close to finding what I looked for—closer than I ever really expected."

Owl Woman was eyeing the pouch in his hand. Now she pointed at it, and Johnny understood the woman wanted a look at it; he passed it over and watched as she examined it in the muted glow of sunlight through canvas. Lame Elk sat as before, still unmoving except for the wobble of his jaw and an occasional twitch of one arthritic hand. From outside came the sounds of the Indian village.

Johnny could make nothing of the look the old squaw gave him, but she didn't offer to return the medicine pouch. Clutching it in strong, work-toughened fingers, she began to talk again and Johnny waited for the girl to interpret; when she remained silent, he glanced at her. "What does she say, Anne?"

To his surprise the girl was frowning, seemingly reluctant to answer. Finally, she said, as though it were being forced from her: "Owl Woman asks you to leave the bag with her a day or two. She's almost certain it's Lame Elk's work. She thinks if, at the right moment, she could show it to him again, it might jog his memory."

"Why, that would be fine!" Johnny Logan quickly grasped at the suggestion. "Tell her yes—of course."

"But, Johnny—"

He didn't even hear Anne's protest. "Tell her anything she's able to learn—anything at all—will mean a lot. And thank her . . ."

The girl did as he'd asked, but her eyes were clouded and her lips tight and suddenly it came home to him that she was really angry. And then she turned abruptly and brushed past him, out of the lodge. Johnny looked at the older woman, in a puzzlement and apology, and hurried after.

Anne had already mounted. When Johnny spoke to her she didn't even look at him but kicked the mare with her heels, evading the reach of his hand as he tried to grab the bridle. Johnny, standing there, watched her ride away from him. He called after her once, then belatedly snatched up the black's ground-tied reins, hit the saddle and went in pursuit.

Stolid, expressionless faces turned to watch them go. Johnny had a bad moment as a naked toddler wandered out in front of the black; he swerved aside just in time. Then the village was left behind and he could lift the black to a gallop, hard after that other rider raising dust across the sun-browned swells of rangeland ahead of him.

CHAPTER VIII

The mare was no match for the black. In minutes the distance had been cut in half. Johnny called the girl's name; she responded at first by kicking her mount to harder effort. Then, as though she saw the futility of it, she pulled in and let him catch up with her. Just to make certain, Johnny reached and got hold of the halter, and both animals came to an uneasy, restless halt.

"Anne!" he exclaimed. "What is it? What's wrong?"

He got a sultry, stabbing look, and without answering she slipped off the back of her pony, leaving him with it, and moved a little way from him. They had halted in a brushy hollow, studded with boulders and a few scrub pine. Anne walked stiffly to a flat rock and seated herself on its edge—strong brown legs thrust out in front of her, her back to Johnny, her eyes lowered to the hands clasped tightly in her lap.

Thoroughly troubled, he snubbed her mare's reins to a branch—he knew the black would stand ground-hitched, like any good cow horse—and then he walked over. Looking down at her, he was able to see only the top of her head and the neat line of parting in the glossy blackness of her hair. He said helplessly, "I don't know what

I did. But whatever it was, I'm sorry—if only you'll *tell* me!"

She raised her head then. Her ripe lower lip was thrust forward in a pout, yet in her eyes he saw now that she was not really angry, but frightened. "Johnny," she said earnestly, "you told me you'd stay on the Reservation only long enough for me to show you Lame Elk's village, and then you'd be leaving—*today*, you said! But now that you've gone and given that pouch to Owl Woman—"

"I see." Just as seriously, Johnny tried to answer. "I've followed kind of a long trail to get here. You must understand how important it is for me, if she can just get the old man to talking; I have to give her every chance. Anyway, I never thought of this as breaking a promise." He smiled, a little lopsidedly. "I didn't know you were that anxious to get rid of me."

The attempt to tease fell through. "I think you know what I'm talking about!" the girl retorted. "Walsh—and Little Wolf, and Strong Runner! By this time, they'll have found out you never went to Piping Rock Agency. They'll be back, looking for you—and how are we ever going to keep you out of their hands, a second time? Don't you see the danger you're in?"

"Of course." Her very evident concern for him brought Johnny down beside her on the rock. He took one of her hands in both of his. "Walsh isn't fooling—I know that," he said quietly and seriously, while her big, dark eyes searched his face. "I'm not making light of it. I'd very much like to know what happened to make him decide he wants me taken prisoner—why it suddenly isn't enough just to have me off the Reservation."

"And you've made up your mind to find out— is that it? You knew, even yesterday, that you were staying—whatever came of your meeting with Lame Elk."

"I'm afraid you're right," he admitted. "I'm still sorry if you're angry about it."

"No—I'm not angry." But she withdrew her hand from his; they sat for a moment without talking or touching. A jay came and perched on a pine-tree limb above their heads, scolded them briefly and then flew off. Stillness settled again.

"What will you do next?" the girl asked.

"About Walsh? I haven't thought that far." He smiled. "I'd say the next thing is to see you home."

Coolly she answered, "Don't put yourself out. *I'm* not in any danger."

"But I like being with you."

She turned to him suddenly. Her face, so close to his own, was sober with concern. "I like it too, Johnny—I like it very much. But I worry about you. I worry a lot! After what they did to you yesterday . . . and *might* have done, if they'd been able to get their hands on you again. . . ."

"Well, so far they haven't. Thanks to you, Anne."

For some reason, a silence fell upon them. The look in the girl's black eyes changed subtly; her mouth, with the ripe underlip, softened. Johnny lifted a hand to touch one of the glossy black braids that framed her face, and then his fingers were on her cheek. At the touch, her full round bosom lifted. And then he had her face cupped between his palms, and he leaned forward and kissed her on the mouth.

She did not try to draw away, but neither did she return the kiss; her eyes remained open, and as he drew back he saw her brows had a pucker of puzzlement between them. It occurred to him suddenly that she didn't know how to kiss! He put his mouth to hers again, gently, and this time her lips responded and he felt the pressure returned.

Johnny was all at once abashed at what he had done—certain that she would be angry. As he dropped his hands and drew back, Anne said primly, "I suppose that's something you learned from all those white girls."

"No," he said seriously. "Not from girls. From my foster mother. I never before tried it with someone my own age."

"Well? And did you like it?"

He couldn't keep from grinning. "Sure! Did you?"

But to that, she gave a very feminine pout and toss of the head. "I don't think you have any business asking!" But Johnny saw a dimple deepen in her cheek and it struck him that what she was doing was flirting.

Johnny caught at her hand. He said, earnestly, "Anne, I *did* like kissing you, and I like our being together. It seems to me there's been something very special about every minute."

She looked straight into his eyes. "I know, Johnny," she said, a little breathlessly. "I've felt it, too." And swiftly she leaned closer and kissed *him,* full on the lips; next moment she had jumped to her feet, drawing her hand from his, and she said in a business-like tone, "But I'm beginning to think it's time we started back."

"All right," Johnny said.

They were both very quiet, now. For his part he was rather shaken by what occurred. He had really had no inkling it was coming, in spite of the strong attraction he knew he felt for this girl. But it had, and nothing could be quite the same afterward. . . .

Subdued and sobered, he went to fetch the girl's pony. He was reaching to free the reins from the pine-branch stub where he had tied them, when there was a brief whirring and stir of air beside his cheek; without warning, a feathered arrow thunked into the tree trunk, missing him by inches.

Johnny Logan whirled and almost stumbled to his knees. He caught his balance, and stared at Swooping Hawk standing in the brush less than twenty feet away, the bow in his hands, a second arrow already nocked to its rawhide string. He could only stare, not sure in that first, heart-stopping instant that the other didn't intend to shoot again. He heard a sound from Anne and knew, without looking at her, that she was frozen motionless as himself.

Then Swooping Hawk lowered the bow slightly, and allowed a scornful smile to lift the corners of his hard mouth. "If you were an enemy," he announced, with mocking humor, "Swooping Hawk's arrow split you open like a melon!"

Johnny Logan swallowed, his constricted throat almost too tight to breathe. "Then I'm mighty glad we're not enemies!" he said. Now that the initial reaction was passing, leaving him shaken, what most affected him was the utter surprise of Swooping Hawk's attack. The man had managed to come, on foot, down a slope choked with dry and rattling brush, and move to within a half dozen yards without making any betraying sound to draw attention to himself. Johnny and the girl, absorbed in each other, had had no hint at all of his presence.

Now Anne found her voice. She said indignantly, "Have you been *spying* on us?"

The young man gave her suggestion a sneer of

utter scorn. "Swooping Hawk? Spy on *you,* Crow Wing? No, I just show this white Indian his ears not sharp enough to challenge Cheyenne."

Johnny had got control of himself now. "The Cheyenne are my own people," he pointed out. "Why should I challenge them?"

"Maybe, to show if you're a coward!"

His tone made Johnny stiffen despite himself, his fists drawing up. He heard a gasp from Anne and then she was saying indignantly, "You have no right to say that! Why, if you knew what he did yesterday—in Walsh's office—"

She subsided when a look from Johnny asked her to. Turning to Swooping Hawk he said flatly, "Whether I happen to be braver or more of a coward than the next fellow is *my* problem, isn't it? I don't see that it concerns you, or anybody else!" Swooping Hawk's obsidian eyes were blank. It plainly wasn't the answer he had expected; putting the matter in those terms was so foreign to a culture based on the supreme importance of physical courage that he was, for a moment, left with nothing to say. And Johnny pressed on:

"I already let you challenge me into a bulldogging contest, and that was silly enough. It stands to reason you've got all kinds of skills I couldn't hope to compete with—but, maybe I've got one or two of my own. But I'm not here to prove anything."

Stubbornly, Swooping Hawk returned to his one theme: "Because you're a coward?"

Johnny let out his breath. "I don't give a damn what you call it. I got no intention of picking a fight with you. I'd rather you were my friend."

"Friend to the white Indian?" Swooping Hawk retorted harshly. "Who takes the road of the enemies of the People?"

"Not every white man is our enemy, Swooping Hawk," Johnny answered with as much patience as he could, anxious to get past the shield of prejudice and hatred. "Maybe it seems like it. But you can't lump together Sid Walsh and someone like Cummings, for instance. Howard Cummings is doing all he can to help. Since the whites will be calling the play, from here out, he thinks the Indian's best chance is to learn all he can about the rules the game is to be played by."

"That's what I've been trying to tell you!" Anne put in. "That's why it's so important that you should come back to school. . . ."

Swooping Hawk looked from one to the other, there in the stillness broken only by the wash of wind in the pines above their heads. Johnny Logan thought for a moment that there was honest doubt and puzzlement in the other man— as though he found himself grappling with notions that were genuinely new. But the moment passed and then something seemed to happen to

Swooping Hawk's eyes; it was like watching a curtain being drawn down.

"Let the white Indian learn from white men!" he snapped, in ringing tones. "Swooping Hawk knows better teachers!"

Suddenly the talk poured out of him, a curious mixture of Cheyenne and badly learned English; still, somehow, because of the eloquence of his gestures Johnny found he could follow the gist of all of it. It was a story Swooping Hawk must have told many times. Talking, the young man strode about the little hollow, through tree shadow and sunlight, brandishing the fist that held the bow, boastfully striking himself on the chest with it.

He told of the time four summers ago, at the moon when the buffalo bulls are rutting; then Jackrabbit, which was his boyhood name, had gone alone to the sacred mountain, to fast and seek the vision that would reveal to him his personal medicine. Two days—three—he waited for a sign from Heammawihio, the Wise One Above, who created the world and all living things. Almost, Jackrabbit despaired. But on the fourth day, when he was weak to the point of lightheadedness, he had been at last granted his vision.

With his own voice, Heammawihio spoke and said: "I send to my son Jackrabbit a messenger, with the medicine that will make him invincible to his enemies. Let Jackrabbit listen, and learn, and remember!"

And on the fifth day the messenger came. It was the hawk, who spoke to Jackrabbit and revealed to him his secrets—what it was that made him more keen of eye than all other creatures, faster of flight than all other birds, sharper of talon in the attack as he dropped upon his prey. And Jackrabbit listened, and watched as the hawk flew before him, demonstrating his skill, wheeling and circling against the sun with the wind singing in his wings. Thus he learned the secret of the hawk's strength in his dive to strike his enemy in mid-air. And when he had prayed in gratitude to Heammawihio, and returned to the village, he was now no longer Jackrabbit but Swooping Hawk—henceforth swift and accurate as his namesake, knowing himself to be unconquerable in battle.

Even the hated white-eyes—and those white Indians like Strong Runner and Little Wolf and the others of Sid Walsh's agency police, who helped in oppressing the Cheyenne—even these would not be spared if the day came when Swooping Hawk turned loose his fury. . . .

The last boastful words were shouted directly at Johnny Logan's face; but to Johnny it was as though he looked across a gulf of ages into those other fanatic, slightly mad eyes. He couldn't doubt that Swooping Hawk believed every word of his story—every detail of his hunger-induced vision, and the powerful medicine it had imparted to him. Even Johnny, because of his blood-heritage from the People, felt a primitive urge to believe in Swooping Hawk's dream. But because of his chance upbringing in a different culture, he knew he did not believe it at all.

Nor was he quite able to disguise his own skepticism. The other must have read it in his eyes; for now Swooping Hawk drew back, his face like iron, as he cried, "The white Indian laughs!"

"No!" Johnny tried to protest. "That's not true!" But Swooping Hawk had already turned his back, and was saying something to Anne—asking her, Johnny guessed from the accompanying gestures, to leave this stranger here and ride with him.

She hesitated, then gave a troubled shake of the head; refused, Swooping Hawk turned sullen. Without another word he swung away, pausing long enough to yank his arrow from the tree. He gave Johnny a last baleful stare, and was gone as swiftly as he had come—up the brushy side of the hollow, his moccasins moving soundlessly. He quickly passed from their view, and a moment later there was the sound of a pony's hoofs starting and then fading away at a brisk run.

Johnny and the girl looked at each other—alone again, but now with the troubling presence of Swooping Hawk somehow still between them.

"I'm sorry," he said gruffly. "I didn't want to get into a quarrel."

"I know," she said. "It wasn't your fault."

"The fellow sure has a chip on his shoulder, when he's around me at least. And I suppose you know why."

Anne nodded. "Because you're Indian—but you dress and talk and think like the white men that he hates."

"There's even more to it than that. He's jealous—of you."

Her dark eyes widened in disbelief. "He despises me! I live in a white man's house—I help teach English to the children. I'm part of the threat to everything he stands for!"

"Oh, I don't doubt he's torn a dozen different ways," Johnny agreed. "But I can see it even if you can't—Swooping Hawk's in love with you, and when he saw us kissing it's a wonder he didn't put that arrow into me instead of into a tree trunk! All his boasting, and the story of his vision—didn't you know that was chiefly for your benefit? He was trying to make up lost ground."

"You honestly think this?" She shook her head, deeply troubled.

"I only hope I can leave here with nothing worse happening between us! The last thing I want to do is fight him—but, worked up the way he is, he may not have it any other way. . . ."

"Johnny, please do your best to keep it from happening!"

He promised solemnly: "You know I will."

But as they mounted and set out through the waning afternoon, in the direction of Cummings', Johnny Logan wondered what chance he had to keep his promise. He didn't think he had heard the last of Swooping Hawk. He thought he could almost feel those hating black eyes; it would be easy for him to imagine the man keeping pace with them as they rode—out of sight, but jealously watching. And biding his time . . .

When they arrived at Cummings', school was just over and the last youngsters were straggling out of the yard, some mounted two or three to a saddleless pony. Entering the log schoolhouse, Johnny and Anne found Cummings sweeping out. The girl said contritely, "Oh, that's *my* job!" and reached to take the broom, but the schoolteacher shook his head as he set it aside. "That can wait," he said. "What did you learn from Lame Elk?"

"Nothing yet," Johnny Logan admitted. Cummings leaned against a corner of his homemade desk, listening carefully to a brief account of their unsatisfactory visit to the old man's lodge, and Johnny's decision to wait for a better time. The schoolteacher's bearded face held a frown that was partly sympathy but, perhaps, partly something else.

"I know you're disappointed," he said slowly, "and I can understand your not wanting it to rest there. I wonder, though . . ." He added, "Did you see anything of the agency police?"

Johnny shook his head. "No." Seeing the concerned look in the other man's eyes he added, "But I think *you* did."

Cummings nodded toward a window. "Earlier this afternoon, I caught sight of a couple of riders watching the place, on that hill yonder. I knew they were police because I saw the sun reflected off their shields."

Quickly Johnny went to the window, to peer at the empty skyline. Eyes narrowed in thought, he demanded, "How long did they stay?"

"A half hour, perhaps. I kept an eye on them; after a while, when I looked again they were gone."

Johnny swore softly. Turning from the window, he saw Anne watching him. "I guess we know what they were looking for," he said gruffly. "I shouldn't even be here. They're suspicious now; it would never do to let them come again and find me here. I'll be riding." He moved toward the door.

Cummings said, behind him, "Where? What do you have in mind?"

He hesitated, looking back. "I'm not sure myself. And the less you really know, the better. We'll be in touch, though," he promised. "In case there should be any word for me from old Lame Elk." He looked at the girl "And I'll be careful."

But when he stepped outside Anne followed him, calling his name. On the steps of the building he waited and she stood close, her face lifted to him, her hand clutching his arm. "You're just going off like this? Without food, even?"

"I carry saddle rations," he assured her. "I'll be fine."

She said slowly, "You're going to the agency, aren't you? I wish you wouldn't! Walsh is a bad man, and he's had his way too long. He can't hold out against the Army, of course—but all the more reason to worry what he might do to *you,* if he gets the chance."

Johnny touched her cheek. "I'll try not to push my luck," he promised. "But somehow or other it looks like I've got the man off balance. I should take advantage of it. I'll be fine," he said again. "Don't worry." And he kissed her.

Anne clung to him briefly, but she let him go when he turned to his waiting horse. In the saddle, he raised a hand in signal. At his last sight of her, she was standing in the doorway of the school, her hands clasped before her, watching him ride away.

He knew it was a picture he would never forget.

CHAPTER IX

Johnny Logan rode first to look at the place Cummings had indicated. Sure enough, there were the marks of the horses—plainly visible where they had moved around as much as their riders would let them, muzzling the sparse bunch grass. Johnny felt certain that if the men had had any real thought of jumping him here and taking him prisoner, they would have kept well out of sight until he appeared. So allowing themselves to be seen—clearly skylined against the grassy hilltop—must have been deliberate, a threat and a warning to the schoolteacher.

Have anything to do with Johnny Logan, and you do it at your own risk . . .

The trail led from here generally westward, in the direction of the agency. Johnny followed it at a leisurely pace, staying off the ridges and keeping a careful watch on the country ahead. When he found a spring bubbling out of some hillside rocks he stopped, loosened the cinch and let the black graze while he had himself a cold meal from the supplies in his saddlebags. He took the opportunity to check his hurts. The facial cuts and swellings were in fair shape, and no longer a bother, but the rib still hurt. The tight bandage beneath his shirt was a help in easing the soreness, and letting him move and breathe without too much discomfort; he left it where it was.

When he rode on, the sun had set and dusk was creeping like smoke out of the hollows, settling across the wide land.

Before he reached the agency, a huge white moon had rolled up into the eastern sky and it paled the firelight shining through the canvas of lodges clustered near the post, the single lantern burning over the closed doorway of the warehouse, the lamplight in the window of Sid Walsh's office. The latter was what interested Johnny Logan. A couple of horses stood at a hitching rack near the building; and if those were the horses he thought they were, then he had reason enough for wanting to know, if he could, what might be going on inside.

After some debate, he nudged the black and started a wide swing to circle the place, holding the animal at a walk and keeping a watchful eye on the agency buildings, that wheeled slowly before him as on a turntable. He came in toward the foot of the rise that loomed behind the agency; here he found a convenient timber thicket and, dismounting, led the black into it. This time, as a precaution, he tied up to a scrub pine, and afterward stood a moment with a hand on the horse's warm flank, listening.

Night wind stirred the branches about him.

Over by the cluster of Indian tepees a dog started barking and another answered it, and his nerves tightened up. He hadn't thought about dogs. . . . But if they stayed where they belonged, and didn't come prowling around the main buildings, he could hope to be able to get in and out again without one of them catching a stranger's scent and raising a cry.

If that should happen, he was in trouble.

He thought of his gun, and drew it to check the loads. Then holstering it again, he started forward, feeling naked and exposed as he stepped out from the trees and into the full glow of the moon.

The warehouse was the nearest building; it would be necessary to pass in back of it. He got close, running lightly to make his crossing of the open as quick as possible and reach the black shadow piled against its wall. A lean-to shanty had been built at one rear corner, and here he caught a faint gleam of lamplight below a pulled window shade; he wondered if that might be the quarters occupied by Sid Walsh's clerk—the sour-faced old man who had sicced Little Wolf on him. The thought made him cautious as he moved toward it, alert for any sound from inside; and when the toe of his boot struck an empty tin and sent it rolling, he froze and sucked in his breath.

But nothing happened, no one gave the alarm.

Convinced that the noise had gone unnoticed he went ahead, circled the lean-to and had the agency building itself directly in front of him. A window of Sid Walsh's office, standing open, made a square of yellow light against its shadowed wall. Johnny Logan ghosted forward, brought up with his shoulders against the logs. He moved along them and so came up beside the opening; and as he halted there, lifting his head to listen without risk of showing himself to those inside, he caught a murmur of voices.

The wall's thickness was such that, even with the open window just inches above his head, he could make little of what he heard. Keenly disappointed, and conscious of every speeding minute, he continued to listen. Someone spoke, someone answered: two voices, though that didn't necessarily mean only two people in the office. Walsh and Little Wolf and Strong Runner, was still his guess. The discussion, whatever it was, seemed lengthy and soberly serious.

And then he was rewarded by hearing, distinctly, his own name spoken with a good deal of heat behind it. The speaker, he felt certain, was Little Wolf. Suddenly the temptation became overwhelming to risk a glance into the room. Poised to raise himself to the level of the sill, Johnny held the movement just in time; without warning the voice of Sid Walsh approached the window—the man was pacing, and now a few words came clearly, together with a distinct gust of cigar smoke: "I still wonder if that damned schoolteacher knows more than he—" The rest of the sentence was lost as Walsh reached the end of his stride and abruptly turned away again.

More indistinguishable talk, then, while Johnny Logan chafed at what he must be missing. At last Little Wolf's voice came again, more loudly: "You want we should—?" But the rest of it was lost to Johnny, as he became suddenly aware of a horseman approaching.

Alarmed, he pulled away from the window and flattened himself into the narrow shadow of the eaves—in time, he hoped.

He'd had only a glimpse of the rider, too brief and too far away to tell him anything. Now, as the horse sounds swelled rapidly, the dogs got noisy again but they seemed satisfied with barking, and quit as the horse came to a halt before the headquarters buildings. Saddle leather creaked, boots struck the gravel; at the same moment the door was thrown open and Johnny heard Sid Walsh call out, in a tone heavy with surprise, "Burkhart! What the devil? You aren't supposed to be here!"

Curiosity outweighed his caution, and brought Johnny up so that he could look past a corner of the screened window. He was staring right at the door as Walsh drew back from it, and the newcomer entered. Burkhart, he saw at once, was one of the troopers who had been with Sergeant Bailey and the major—a man with reddish hair and a narrow jaw that gave his face something of a foxy, tapered look. He pulled off his campaign hat, batted it against the edge of the door and knocked dust from it in a small cloud. Evidently he had been some hours in the saddle; he looked tired and short-tempered.

He told the agent, "Sarge sent me with word of the cattle. It'll be delivered at Bull Flat, probably sometime before noon tomorrow."

"Tomorrow!" Johnny saw Walsh's head jerk back at this news. "It wasn't to be until next week!"

The trooper shrugged. "Change of plans. McCord put his herd on the trail yesterday; he'd already come near half way when we run into him."

Sid Walsh was angry. "I guess I know what this means! The herd's in even worse shape than McCord let on—now he's anxious to unload. No concern to him, or to Bailey either, that *I'm* the one who could get stuck. By God, I don't think I like it!"

"No use bitching to me," Burkhart told him indifferently. "I only carry messages."

The agent scowled in silence for a moment; Johnny saw him paw at the thick burnsides, with the hand that held his fuming cigar. "Where's the major?" he demanded finally.

141

"Started back to the fort, soon as he finished his business at Piping Rock. He took Rogers with him, sent me and Sarge with final word to McCord that he'd been okayed for the beef contract."

Sid Walsh muttered something, still scowling, and shoved the cigar into his thin-lipped trap of a mouth. "*Damn* McCord!" he muttered in a blue spurt of smoke. "Bailey, too! I've been leery of this deal of theirs, from the time they first put it to me. It's damned dangerous!"

"According to Bailey," the trooper said, "your cut ought to more than make it worth your while."

"He says that, does he?"

Burkhart moved his shoulders indifferently. "Well, I brought the message I was told to. What word do you want me to take back?"

Glowering at him, Sid Walsh puffed a furious cloud of smoke from the cigar clamped between his jaws. And it was in that moment that Johnny Logan heard the scrape of a footstep, just behind him.

He stiffened, starting to turn, and freezing as something hard was rammed against his back. A nervous voice said sharply, "Don't turn—don't move at all! This is a shotgun!"

His own voice, when he managed to speak, sounded to him like a hoarse croak. "All right. Just be careful, will you?"

"*You* be careful!" Johnny thought now he recognized the voice, and the thread of nervous tension he heard in it made the cold sweat start. "Both these barrels are loaded. Now, just raise your hands."

"I'm doing it!" He obeyed quickly, anxious at any cost not to make the holder of the shotgun any more nervous than he already was.

It was the clerk, of course—the gray-haired man whose bony fingers were better suited to holding a pen, or turning the pages of a ledger. He sounded rattled and excitable, and Johnny knew there was nothing much more dangerous than a weapon in the hands of a nervous amateur.

The light from the window was partly blocked now by a man's head and shoulders. Sid Walsh demanded, "Who's out there?"

"It's me, Sid," answered the clerk. "Archer . . . I just caught this fellow under your window— spying. I'm bringing him in."

He would have been smarter, Johnny Logan thought, to hold his prisoner there while someone came out to get him. In his inexperience, it apparently did not even occur to him to take the pistol out of Johnny's holster.

Still, with the twin muzzles of that shotgun right against his spine, a man would have to be a fool to take chances, when a single touch of a finger against a trigger was certain to blow him in two. Johnny Logan let the shotgun prod him away from the window and start him forward, around the corner to the front of the building. Other guns were waiting in the door for him, and as he was marched into the lamplight he heard Walsh's sharp sound of recognition. Hands seized Johnny, thrust him roughly across the threshold so that he tripped and nearly fell. He felt the tug at his belt as the gun was slipped from its holster. He caught his balance and stood, helpless and surrounded by his enemies.

There were four of them—Johnny had expected to find Strong Runner here, as well, but he'd been wrong: The man wasn't in the room. Little Wolf and the trooper, Burkhart, had put up their own guns, but Sid Walsh had Johnny's pistol and he held it like a man who knew how to handle one. It was the shotgun that still bothered Johnny the most—the hands that held it trained on him were white-knuckled with the tightness of their grip, and now he could see the clerk's face and the man looked a little wild-eyed. He also looked quite pleased with himself as, stammering, he explained what had happened:

"I heard a noise outside my room, and when I looked there he was, sneaking past, plain as anything in all that moonlight. So I went and got the shotgun, and there he was under your window—so interested in what he was listening to, all I had to do was walk up and shove the thing in his back."

Sid Walsh's black eyes bored into the prisoner. "Very good, Archer—good work. We'll be careful of him. But you'd better keep your eyes open. He may have friends."

"Don't worry!" Archer patted the stock of his weapon. "They won't get past this!" A nod from Walsh dismissed him, and a moment later the clerk was gone. The screen rattled shut behind him.

A hand seized Johnny by the front of his jacket, hauled him around to meet Walsh's stare that was like splintered glass. "You damned sneaking redskin!" the agent gritted, between tight lips. "This time you've pushed your luck too far!"

"I thought Sarge left instructions for you to haul him in and keep hold of him," Burkhart said. "Why was he still running loose?"

Walsh shrugged irritably. "Not my fault. I got the word too late—by then I'd already had him beaten up and kicked off the Reservation."

"Looks like the lesson didn't take." The trooper narrowly regarded Johnny's face, still marked by the fists that worked him over. "What does he think he's up to, snooping outside your office?"

"That," Sid Walsh promised grimly, "is something I intend to get out of him. You go tell Bailey, little as I like the idea, I'll see him and McCord on Bull Flat. You also tell him, if anything goes wrong I won't end up holding the sack!"

"I'll tell him," Burkhart said shortly. His eyes

sought Johnny's face again. "And I'll tell him you got the Injun. You better be sure and hang onto him this time! He gave Bailey some personal trouble, down at Spellman's. The way Sarge has been talking, I think he's going to want another crack at him for that."

He strode out, then, pulling on his campaign hat. A moment later there was the sound of his horse starting up and heading away, in the direction from which he'd ridden earlier. That faded, and the silence of the summer night descended again.

Alone with Little Wolf and the agent, Johnny Logan stood waiting. For the moment Sid Walsh seemed to be paying him little attention; he had fallen to pacing again, his boots loud on the puncheon floor of the office, smoke spurting furiously from the cigar clamped between his jaws. He was still brooding, Johnny thought, over the news Burkhart had brought him, roiling emotions reflected in his scowl that made the narrow face ugly with anger. When at last, with a shrug, he turned again to the prisoner, it was as though the problem of Johnny Logan was a distraction that he resented being bothered with.

He dropped into his swivel chair, tilted it back and laid Johnny's gun on the desk beside him. His fingers drummed soundlessly on the butt of it; the oil lamp burning on the desk cast odd shadows across his face, deepening the eye sockets and giving them a satanic cast. "All right, Logan," the agent said. "If that's the name you go by . . . You're a nervy bastard, but you're not the first troublemaker of your race that I've had to deal with. I've broken tougher ones than you! Do you believe that?"

Johnny merely looked at him, answering by neither word nor by change of expression. He had the satisfaction of seeing Walsh's face darken, his eyes harden with irritation.

"By God," the man breathed. "I think perhaps you don't understand just what you're up against! And that's partly my fault, because I was too easy on you the first time." The swivel chair creaked as he sat forward suddenly. A hand rose to stab a pointing finger.

"You've got a few things to get through that skull of yours," Sid Walsh snapped. "You got to realize you're all alone, boy—and I mean, *alone!* There's just one law here, and it's mine. I can do absolutely anything I like with you—you can disappear completely, and there isn't a soul that will know the difference."

"Maybe," Johnny Logan retorted. "And maybe not." He could have bitten his tongue out the moment it was said, for he saw the sudden interest with which the other man snapped that up.

"Then you're *not* alone!" Walsh interpreted, and his eyes gleamed and his lips pulled away

147

from his teeth in the start of a grin. "I wondered if you would admit it! Who are you working with, Logan? Who was your drunken friend that brought you back onto the Reservation and tried to beg shells for his gun off the schoolteacher. Or—" he paused "—did Cummings invent some of that? Is he in this—deeper than he'd like me to know?"

Johnny tried to control his features. The last thing he wanted was to bring suspicion on anyone at the school; he had to say something and he blurted—rather lamely he thought, "You've got a good imagination!"

That killed the agent's grin. His mouth instantly fell into wicked lines, and his cold eyes flicked away from the prisoner briefly. It must have been a signal to Little Wolf that Johnny failed to catch—he was totally unprepared when a fist like a club struck him on the side of his neck where it joined the jaw hinge. Agony welled in his throat and he was driven sideward, staggering; he would have fallen, had Little Wolf not caught him by the arm and held him firmly.

For a moment his eyes went out of focus and there seemed to be two of Sid Walsh seated in the glow of the desk lamp, glaring up at him. He blinked and shook his head a little to clear it.

"Now, you listen to me!" said Walsh, and his voice was like the crack of a whip. "Here's the way I make it out: When you sneaked back onto the Reservation yesterday, you had it in mind to follow Major Harriman up to Piping Rock, and give him an earful about the McCord deal. Haven't I got it right? *Haven't I?*" he repeated furiously.

Johnny blinked. He almost said, *How could I have told him, when absolutely all I know is what I just heard out there under your window?* The fist landed once more, this time sinking into his ribs and filling him with agony as it struck the one that had been injured by the toe of a cowhide boot. His knees sagged. Again it was the grip on his arm that kept him upright.

"*Did* you tell him?" Sid Walsh was almost shouting. "Was it Harriman sent you back here tonight to try for more information?" And then the man's temper snapped completely and he told Little Wolf, between his teeth, "Make him answer!"

Johnny understood, then, what was going to happen to him.

As Little Wolf hauled his victim around to face him, there was amusement and knowledge of power in the gleam of the black eyes; a fist was already cocked and ready to strike another punishing blow. But a man couldn't let himself be docilely beaten unconscious. Johnny Logan, spurred by desperation, was ready. He allowed the jerk at his arm to give him momentum, and his other fist swung around and struck his tormentor squarely in the face, taking him across one eye and the bridge of the nose.

It was unexpected and, even without much steam behind it, must have hurt; Little Wolf grunted and gave back a step, losing his grip on Johnny and blinking against sudden blinding tears. Johnny used what little advantage this gave him, though his knees were unsteady and his whole body was filled with the hurt of that damaged rib. He waded ahead, arms swinging. One fist struck Little Wolf in the chest and he felt the metal shield under his knuckles; with the other he tried for the jaw but managed to do no more than graze it, without force.

And then a crushing blow struck him on the side of the head and staggered him. As stars exploded behind his eyes, Little Wolf swung again and this time took him in the chest, cutting off his wind, sending him stumbling helplessly backward.

There was a hoarse shout from Sid Walsh, somewhere just behind him. Johnny's hurtling body struck the edge of the desk where Walsh was seated, hard enough to jar the heavy piece of furniture. Hurled part way around, doubled over, he found the heat and glare of the blazing kerosene lamp directly in front of his face and instinctively flung up a protecting hand. And, half blinded, he caught a glimpse of his own revolver lying on the desk where Walsh had laid it.

Too dazed for thinking, he acted. The edge of his fist struck the base of the lamp a blow that swept it in Walsh's direction. He heard the agent's sudden cry of alarm, and the squeal of the swivel chair as he backed hastily away from the lamp hurtling into his lap. Then there was the crash of its glass chimney breaking, and the room plunged abruptly into darkness.

Groping over the littered desk, Johnny's fingers located the hard metal of his gun. In trying to seize the handle he batted it away, set it spinning on the felt; then trapped it again and managed to snatch it up. The office was a hubbub, now, with Walsh and Little Wolf yelling back and forth in the sudden darkness. Gripping his gun, Johnny Logan had wits enough to spin away from the desk and sink to a crouch, making a smaller target if someone should begin shooting.

The after-image of the lamp, seared into his vision, flickered in front of him wherever he turned his head; but now, in spite of it, he could see the front door standing open—an oblong opening filled with the glow of moonlight outside, beyond the screen. It occurred to him that he was nearer that door than either of his enemies—also, that if he meant to move it would have to be fast.

He didn't allow time to think. He gathered himself, and suddenly hurtled toward the door, staying low. At once a gun roared, its report an ear-punishing thunderclap against the walls and low roof, and briefly lighting the darkness with its muzzle flash. But the shot missed his lunging shape; next instant, ears ringing, he struck the screen door with head and shoulder and batted it aside and went through the opening. He tripped and went rolling in the dirt, pain stabbing at his hurt rib. Then, catching himself, he reared onto his knees and quickly triggered off two shots, directly at the door.

After that, somehow he was on his feet, still dazed and not yet breathing right from Little Wolf's sledging blows; and he was running.

CHAPTER X

He was staggering slightly, hurting at every step as he headed for the rear of the building, on the shortest course for the place where he had left the black; the gun dragged at him heavily as it swung in his fist. Behind him there was shouting and now he thought he heard the screen door squeal and slap shut again, knew that pursuit was after him.

Over at the Indian lodges, the dogs were barking their heads off. The uproar in Walsh's office had split the night apart.

As he veered to circle past the rear of the warehouse, Johnny Logan halted abruptly at sight of a pair of men standing just at the lean-to corner. They showed clearly in the flood of moonlight: One, he thought, was Archer—the clerk; the other, from his silhouette, might be Strong Runner. They were looking directly at him, and he caught the faint gleam of the shotgun's tubes in Archer's hands. For a heartbeat, no one did more than stare. Then, from behind Johnny, came Sid Walsh's shout: "*Stop him!* Kill him if you have to. . . ."

That jarred them all loose. The shotgun lifted, and Strong Runner took a step forward with a revolver showing now in his fist. Johnny Logan tipped up the muzzle of his own pistol and flung a shot their way, hoping to rattle them; at the same moment, knowing he was stopped from reaching his horse, he veered in a new direction. A six-gun blast answered his shot but in this deceptive light the bullet came nowhere near.

Just ahead was the bare ridge that lifted behind the agency buildings. Here at its foot, the ground roughed up into erosion gullies and was spotted with chunks of boulder fallen from its side; this offered his best and nearest hope of cover, and Johnny wasted no time making for it. There was another shot behind him, then two at once—he could only guess how many guns were on hand for Walsh to throw after him. But a running target made poor shooting, and as yet no one had managed to score though the muscles of his shoulders locked tight in expectation.

Then the nearest boulder was within reach, low brush around it. He ran straight into the brush, lifting his legs high and plowing ahead despite the branches that snagged his clothing and tried to hold him back. Johnny Logan trampled and smashed through it frantically, and suddenly he was free of the stuff and he dived into the boulder's protection. He crouched there panting, his ribs aching, sweat smarting in the scratches he had collected on his face and the backs of his hands; and a bullet struck the rock and screamed off somewhere into the night. For the moment he was safe, but he hunched his shoulders involuntarily.

Palm pressed against his ribs, he waited for his breathing to settle and the pain and shakiness to subside. After that he had to give attention to his revolver, punching out the empties and replacing them with fresh shells from his belt. As he worked he was listening for any sound to tell him what his enemies were up to. Once his hands went still as he heard a voice that must belong to Archer, the clerk: "Don't let him into those trees. I think he left his horse there somewhere."

Johnny Logan grimaced, at that—it meant they had him cut off, and pinned down, and that they knew it.

He rocked the cylinder back into place. He had left his hat on the floor of Walsh's office; he shoved the hair back from his sweaty face and then, holding the gun ready, cautiously raised himself for a look across the boulder. As he did so, the light flickered and went dim. Puzzled, Johnny tilted his head for a look at the sky and discovered that, unknown to him, clouds had been building up—a sheet of them, moving out of the north, with misty outriders scudding filmily ahead. Now, as one of these obscured the moon's face briefly, the night seemed to turn sensibly colder; the wind picked up, rattling in the brush and whipping the hair into Johnny's face and covering other sounds. The clouds shuttled on and the moon brightened; looking toward the agency Johnny saw the shadows change. The buildings stood out briefly, then pulled back once more into darkness.

He shifted his grip on the gun, made uneasy by this ebbing of light and shadow in which shapes seemed to melt and flow indistinctly. He hunted for his enemies that he knew must be there somewhere, and couldn't tell if any movement he saw was actual, or imagined; while the dry rattling of brush confused him and baffled his attempt to listen. Except for the continued barking of an aroused dog at the Indian lodges, there was no sound he could put a name to.

Maybe they were waiting, prepared to cut him down as he tried to reach his horse; by this time they could have found the black and removed it, knowing that on foot he should be easy to run to earth. Thinking about that, he suddenly remembered the animals he had seen tied to a hitching post near the headquarters building. Yes, there was an outside chance, he thought—but only if Walsh's men were too confident. It was just possible he could fool them, reach one of those horses and in the deceptive play of moon and shadow, make his getaway.

Anything seemed better than staying helpless where he was.

He gathered his legs under him—and the voice

to his right and a little behind him said softly, "You move . . . I shoot."

Every muscle bunched. Slowly, Johnny brought his head around and saw the figure standing a half dozen yards from him, a revolver aimed at his unprotected back. It was incredible, that in such short time the man could have circled and come in on his blind side, making no sound at all, taking him completely unaware. But then the rags of cloud drew away from the moon's face and the man leaped into clear outline. It was Strong Runner.

There was heavy amusement in his voice as he spoke again. "You not hard to fool!" And then, his voice taking on a hard edge: "Drop your gun!"

Johnny could not bring himself to, because that would be the end of it. Stiff muscles in his neck began to ache as he peered, head sharply twisted, across his shoulder at the man who held him helpless. If the moon would only go behind another cloud . . . just long enough . . . But, perversely, its round white disk seemed now to have swum clear, into an open patch of stars and black sky.

Strong Runner's patience was fraying. "The gun—or I blow you in two!"

There was a sudden faint whisper of sound. Strong Runner's whole body gave a jerk and his head rocked back, and Johnny saw a glint of something projecting from the front of his throat. Incredulous, Johnny Logan watched him buckle at the knees and then, dropping his unfired gun, fold slowly to the ground.

A few yards beyond him Swooping Hawk lowered his bow, and Johnny and he looked at one another across the body of the dead policeman. Breaking free then of the paralysis of shock that held him, Johnny Logan went to look down at Strong Runner, shuddering as he saw how the moon shone full on his staring eyes and gaping jaw, and on the point of the arrow that impaled his throat.

Then Swooping Hawk had joined him, and Johnny found his voice.

"Where did you come from?" he demanded in bewilderment. "Maybe I wasn't imagining it, after all, when I couldn't get it out of my head that you were trailing me. But—this!" He indicated the body at their feet. "You saved my life . . . and I'm damned if I know why!"

He could read nothing at all in that other face. Swooping Hawk looked down at the one he had killed. He nudged the limp body, with the toe of a moccasin. He said roughly, "Strong Runner was traitor to the People."

"He sold out to Sid Walsh, all right," Johnny agreed. "If you figure that made him your enemy—him, and Little Wolf, and the others that pinned on the agency badges."

But it was not a time for talking. Swooping Hawk gave a summoning jerk of the head. "Come!"

"And leave it like this?" Johnny Logan exclaimed. "With your arrow in him? If Walsh can identify it, and trace this kill to you—he'll see you hang!"

He actually thought, for a moment, Swooping Hawk intended it as a gesture of defiance. But then, with an eloquent shrug, the other turned back and went down on his knees beside Strong Runner and rolled the body over. Johnny Logan looked quickly away; trying not to listen, he nevertheless heard the snap as the shaft was broken in two, and a moment later Swooping Hawk rose to his feet and Johnny saw the bloodied pieces of the arrow in his hand, and swallowed hard. Swooping Hawk ordered shortly, "Get horse." He walked away, leaving the other standing there.

For just an instant Johnny remembered his thought about trying for one of the agency mounts. But that had been a desperate notion at best, and now with Strong Runner removed, the odds against him were lowered. As he hesitated, he looked up and saw that a considerable sheet of cloud was advancing steadily across the sky. Suddenly the moon's face was swallowed up; darkness engulfed the night. It was all the chance he needed, and Johnny Logan started at a run toward the trees where he had left the black. He could only hope it hadn't been moved.

A cry sounded, to his left; he thought it was the clerk, Archer, and instinct made him dive flat to the earth seconds ahead of a smashing report, and a tearing burst of flame. Hugging the ground, he heard the whistle of buckshot and then spent missiles were pattering to the earth like rain, all around him. At once he was up again, digging with his boots to get quick speed. The trees showed blackly, just yards ahead. He lunged toward them. There was more shouting; the shotgun let go with its other barrel. Lead pellets raked the bole of a pine, right at his elbow, but then Johnny was into the trees and miraculously unhurt.

Still, someone might be in here waiting and he had his gun ready. No challenge met him, however. He heard faint movement and bore toward it, and here was the horse precisely where he had left it, all but invisible in thick darkness. He found the reins, jerked them free and felt for the stirrup. The black must have smelled fear on him and for a moment was upset, moving around uneasily. Johnny quieted it with a word, and swung quickly up. He held himself low in the saddle to avoid low-lying branches, as he pointed away from the agency buildings.

Then he was out of the trees, and here was Swooping Hawk mounted on his own spotted pony. He called softly, and Johnny Logan answered, and followed as the other promptly started away.

Plunging into darkness after bright moonlight, Johnny was riding blind and could do no more than try to guide on the faint glimpses he had of the other rider, trusting to the black to find footing. They began to climb, loose rock turning occasionally underfoot; it occurred to him that they were on a trail of some sort, cutting across a flank of the ridge that lifted in back of the agency. This was confirmed presently as the ground dropped away again; they hit flat country and kept riding, bearing north, putting distance behind them.

At last Swooping Hawk halted and Johnny Logan pulled up beside him. They both studied the way they had come, testing the windy night. Swooping Hawk grunted at last and said, "No one follows. You leave now."

Johnny looked at him, trying to read his face in the darkness. "Leave the Reservation?" he said. "Or—leave Anne? That's what you really mean, isn't it?"

"Crow Wing no white Indian's squaw!"

The angry outburst told Johnny what he wanted to know—that, and the pointed way in which Swooping Hawk refused to speak the girl's adopted white name. Johnny, frowning, was slow to answer as he carefully chose his words. "The last thing in the world I want," he said finally, "is to get in a row with you, especially over Anne. For one thing, neither of us has any right. And besides that, I owe you too much. I said once before, I'd like to be friends . . . and that was before you'd gone and saved my life for me. But, it's up to you . . ."

He paused, but Swooping Hawk neither spoke nor moved, during a long moment while the horses grew restless, with the night wind pressing against them. Seeing that the other was adamant, Johnny Logan shook his head resignedly and picked up the reins.

"One last thing I'd like to ask you—it has nothing to do with Anne . . . I've heard mention of a place called Bull Flat. Can you tell me where it is?" He thought for a moment he would not get even that much, but then Swooping Hawk's arm lifted in a curt pointing movement, toward the southwest, and again dropped to his side. "It's inside the Reservation boundary?" Johnny prodded, and thought he saw a brief nod.

He drew a breath. "Look! There's one thing you could do—not for me, but for yourself— and all the Cheyenne." Getting no reaction, he plowed ahead: "Maybe you've heard that a rancher named McCord had been awarded the contract for the Reservation beef ration. The reason I asked about Bull Flat, I just learned tonight, in Walsh's office, that Nels McCord will be delivering a herd there, sometime before noon tomorrow. There's something very much wrong with that herd! Just what, I don't know; but for some reason, Sid Walsh thinks I do—and that's the reason he wants me put out of the way.

"Whatever crooked work is going on," he continued, while Swooping Hawk listened without any kind of response, "that Army sergeant, Ed Bailey, is mixed up in it along with Walsh and McCord; on the other hand, Bailey's boss— Major Harriman—knows nothing about it at all. If he did, he'd stop it. It's my feeling that that herd has somehow got to be kept off the Reservation—even if it means some shooting!

"Harriman's gone back to Fort Dilson, and it leaves us only one man who might be in a position to help: Arne Jenson, who *was* supplying the beef until McCord underbid him, strikes me as a fair man, and he has a crew to back him up. If McCord is really trying to put something over on the Army, at the Cheyenne's expense, then I think Jenson would do whatever he can for us. At least," Johnny said, "I think it's worth my while to try finding his ranch and having a talk with him. Meanwhile, what I'd like you to do is get word to Howard Cummings, for him to relay to the fort."

He paused, still looking in vain for some sign that his words were registering. A little desperate now—and also a little angry—he pressed harder:

"Look! You got to understand, this is the Army's business. Harriman gave McCord his contract, and only he can cancel it; what's more, it's important for him to know his sergeant is making crooked deals behind his back. I think Cummings is the man who'd have the best chance of convincing him he should look into it. Will you go see Cummings, while I'm hunting up Arne Jenson?"

Johnny wished he could see the other's face more clearly, to try and read in it whatever lay behind his continuing silence. Then Swooping Hawk made a short, chopping gesture with one hand. He said curtly, "The white Indian can carry his own messages!"

"Damn it!" Johnny exclaimed. "It's no favor to *me!* Can't you get it through your head, I'm asking you to do something to help your own people. . . ." But he saw it was useless. Swooping Hawk had already jerked his pony's head around and was riding away from him—and clearly, he wasn't headed in the direction of the school. Johnny called after him once, angrily; then he let it go, with a shake of the head.

The windy darkness closed down, and he was alone.

So much for that. It had probably been foolish to think the jealous and hostile Swooping Hawk—even if he had saved Johnny Logan's life—would be willing to take Johnny's orders.

Anything that was to be done, he would have to do himself. He was as certain as ever that Jenson was the logical person to ask for help, but on the other hand, word must somehow definitely reach Major Harriman; yet he couldn't be in two places at once.

Johnny debated the problem—the time he had, and the probable distances he would have to cover. He had only a vague idea of the location of Arne Jenson's ranch, but he knew he was somewhere between it and the Cummings place—perhaps halfway between. Anyhow you sliced it, it meant he had some steady riding and doubling back on his tracks to do, that wouldn't have been necessary had Swooping Hawk been willing to help.

Still, with any luck, he should be able to make it and reach both places in time. He told his horse, "Sorry, but I don't know when either of us is going to get a chance to rest, for a while yet." He swung his bridles to the east, and gave the horse its head. The black had already carried him considerable distances since daylight; he let it fall of its own accord into a pace that it could maintain, and cover the miles they still had to travel.

It was still a good deal short of midnight when he came in on the log buildings of the school and the Cummings home, but he found them dark, with no lights showing—these people evidently kept regular hours. He moved stiffly as he threw his leg over and dismounted, feeling the effect of the long day's riding on top of the physical punishment he had taken.

He must have been heard riding up. He had no more than lifted his fist to knock when the door opened by Howard Cummings, in trousers and a nightshirt and carpet slippers and holding a lighted lamp. "Why, Johnny!" the schoolteacher exclaimed, looking at the man who stood bare-headed in front of him. "What is it? Is something wrong?"

Johnny Logan pushed his fingers through the tangle of black hair. "Can I talk to you?"

"Of course! Come in—come in!"

He was inside then, and a moment later both Ella Cummings and Anne appeared fastening the robes they had hastily put on. The girl had let down her lustrous black hair and it lay soft about her shoulders—Johnny Logan could scarcely take his eyes off her. Studying his face, in turn, her dark eyes were troubled. "Are you all right?" she demanded anxiously, and he quickly assured her that he was.

They seated him at the kitchen table and a cup of coffee, steaming from the pot that was kept heating at the back of the stove, appeared in front of him. Johnny Logan drank it gratefully, letting it clear some of the fog of weariness from his head.

He put down the cup, and looked around at the

faces anxiously watching him. "I'll make this as short as possible," he said. "I've just been to the agency. . . ."

"I knew it!" Anne broke in. "I begged you not to."

He smiled a little. "You can see, nothing happened to me." Under no circumstances did he intend to alarm her, by letting her know what a narrow escape he had actually had there. He looked at the schoolteacher. "Mr. Cummings, I learned some things I wasn't supposed to know. I want to see what you think about it."

The other man nodded soberly. He said, "I'm listening. . . ."

Johnny Logan talked. They heard him out in silence; Howard Cummings, usually so mild of manner, turned grim and his eyes hardened. Interrupting at last, he said, "Let me understand this. Are you saying you think this is a *diseased* herd Nels McCord is bringing onto the Reservation?"

"Not only that, but in such bad condition that he can't wait to dump them. Sid Walsh is almost ready to panic—afraid of the deal, afraid of getting stuck; but now that the Army's stripped him of his chances for graft he'll have no choice but to go through with this one. As usual, the last thing anyone's concerned about is the Cheyenne—fed poisoned beef, the grass on their Reservation contaminated . . ."

"But, just a minute!" Cummings insisted. "I've met this Major Harriman—he seemed to me like a good man. Didn't you say he'd seen McCord's herd, and approved it?"

"He saw the herd. It's my guess this one's being rung in, in its place. Harriman's returned to Fort Dilson; Sergeant Bailey will accept delivery on behalf of the Army. And Bailey is part of the deal—he'll sign the papers, McCord will be vouchered for payment. The two of them, and Sid Walsh, will split the profit from cattle that otherwise would have to be destroyed, for a total loss. The Army—and the Cheyenne—will be left holding the sack."

Fingers silently drumming the table, the school-teacher frowned as he thought over Johnny's story. Suddenly he slapped his palm flat against the wood. "You've convinced me," he said. "This must be looked into. I'm a fair horseman. It's sixty miles to the fort; but if I ride all night, get a change of mounts at Cottonwood Station, I should make it by morning. I'm sure I can get Harriman—or someone else if he isn't there—to listen to me." He got to his feet. "I'll get dressed, and saddle up. I'll take care of your horse, while I'm at it."

"No need of that," Johnny Logan said quickly.

"But you're staying the night, surely? You look thrashed out."

Johnny stood up. "I've got more riding to do,

myself. Even if you can get help at the fort, the distance is too great. You'll never have them here in time to stop that herd, before it's delivered and signed for."

"Likely not," the schoolteacher agreed. "But I don't see any permanent harm. Walsh and McCord, and their sergeant friend, will never get away with this now. There'll be an investigation. If the cattle are diseased, they'll be destroyed and a charge of fraud brought."

"To hang on forever in the courts," Johnny pointed out. "And meanwhile, what happens to the Cheyenne? I've seen how this works! Right now there's a warehouse full of shoddy goods and spoiled food, piled up there by Walsh—and Harriman himself told me it all has to be used up somehow, before it can be replaced with better. Once that herd's been accepted—even if it's destroyed—do you honestly think the Cheyenne will see another pound of beef until every single head has been written off the books? That will take months. They can go hungry, or starve, for all the white man cares!"

Before the challenge of his angry stare, Howard Cummings was forced to drop his own. "I won't insist you're wrong," he said in a tired voice. "I've seen too many things happen that made me ashamed my skin is white! But what can *you* do, Johnny Logan?"

"By myself, nothing. But there's a man named

Arne Jenson, who stands to lose if McCord's herd reaches its destination—the rancher that beef contract rightly belongs to. I intend to find out what he has to say about this."

"I see," Cummings murmured, after a pause. Troubled, his gaze rested on the younger man. "Yes, Jenson might want to help—if only for selfish reasons, in order to hold the market for his own beef. But aren't you afraid, if he tries to stop McCord tomorrow, there's apt to be shooting? Men can be hurt—perhaps killed!"

Johnny met his look, directly. "The Cheyenne have been hurt, Mr. Cummings. They've been tricked and beaten, and stripped of the power to fight for themselves. I'm a Cheyenne; when it comes down to it, they're my people. If I can keep this one wrong from being done them, I'm afraid I can't worry too much about a few white men getting killed!"

He knew they were shocked by his words, but once spoken he couldn't take them back. He looked at Ella Cummings, mumbled his thanks for the coffee, and then abruptly he turned and left them. Somehow he couldn't let himself look at Anne. He didn't want to see, just then, what feelings might have been reflected in her eyes.

CHAPTER XI

In spite of what he had said about riding directly to look for Arne Jenson, in actual fact Johnny Logan rode only a few hundred yards to a timbered knoll which gave him a good view of the Cummings' place. There he picketed the black, offsaddled, and broke out his blankets. He made himself comfortable with his back against a pine trunk, and settled down to watch the house.

He hadn't forgotten Sid Walsh making threats against Howard Cummings, trying to force him to admit a connection with the schoolteacher. If he was really set on running Johnny to earth, Walsh might very possibly send his men looking here for him—in which case Johnny Logan would much prefer to be in the open instead of trapped inside the house. And if there *was* danger he certainly couldn't ride away and leave these people to face it alone, especially knowing he himself would be the cause of it.

The night was busy with wind pummeling the trees about him. Only a dim brightness showed where the moon made its way through the swift-moving cloud cover; otherwise, darkness was absolute except for the glow of lighted windows yonder. Presently the house door opened and Howard Cummings stepped out. He vanished in the direction of the horse shed, reappeared moments later mounted for the trail. He started off at a good strong, reaching gait—like a man who intended to be several hours in the saddle, and cover a good deal of distance. The sound of hoofbeats quickly faded. A little while afterward, the lights in the house were put out and then Johnny was alone with the dark, and the horse cropping the grass nearby, and his silent vigil.

As the night grew older, heavy thoughts began to weigh on him—thoughts of that last angry outburst, about not caring too much if he were to see a few white men die: Those had been cruel words to hurl at someone like Howard Cummings, a white man and, surely, Johnny Logan's friend. He knew Anne had been shocked to hear them. And they made him wonder, more than ever, about himself.

How close did he really feel toward these people on the Reservation—was his anger from the blood, or only a natural sympathy for anyone being mistreated and taken advantage of? After all, the color of a man's skin made him neither a devil, nor a saint . . . as Johnny should know as well as anyone. He mustn't forget that tonight Strong Runner had died, violently, and probably deserving it—and Strong Runner had been a Cheyenne, a traitor to his race.

What it came down to, finally, was simply this: The long battle for possession of a continent had dragged to its close. The red man had lost to a stronger enemy, who now considered it his rightful turn at land he thought he could put to better use than the Indian could. That might or might not be so; Johnny Logan, with a foot in both worlds, thought he could understand both points of view, especially after these few glimpses of what reservation life had done to the Cheyenne. But seeing both sides didn't necessarily make it easier for a man to know where he belonged. It could make him an outsider to both . . .

An hour passed, another; weariness took its toll. Satisfied at last that Sid Walsh was not planning any move against his friends, Johnny Logan settled into his blanket and allowed himself the luxury of sleep.

He was up an hour before dawn, assembling his gear. The cloud sheet had moved on; the moon had set but the stars were deep and glittering, and a predawn wind carried the scent of pine and grass. Johnny Logan walked about, stretching the cramps out of chilled muscles and testing the state of that damaged rib—it seemed to be doing well enough, within its tight bandage, and he found he could move about almost free of pain. A last look at the Cummings place showed everything quiet and apparently normal. Johnny mounted and turned down the far side of the knoll. He chewed on a strip of jerky from his pack as he rode west, retracing his course of the night before. The sky paled, the world freshened with dawn.

He got into a patch of ground fog, built up from mists rising off the shallow meander of a stream—like cotton, gray and chill, muffling sound. It clung ghostlike among the black trees that marched away to his left, up a rise mounting to a steep fault rim. In this thick stillness, he and the black could have been the only living things within miles. And yet, as they moved through it, Johnny found himself suddenly holding his breath, conscious of an unexplained feeling of near danger.

Then, to a freakish shift of air currents, the mist shook and lifted like a curtain. And not a hundred yards in front of Johnny, it revealed the figure of a horseman approaching at a walk, his body bent to study the ground. Stuck in the band of his black felt hat was a single eagle feather.

Johnny Logan's breath caught in his throat. He didn't have to be told whose trail Little Wolf was following—or what would have happened if, in another minute, they had met head-on in the enveloping fog. As it was, for a moment he had the advantage; Little Wolf, intent on his tracking, had still not looked up. Johnny had hurriedly drawn his gun, but he balked at the idea of using it on an enemy without warning; on the other hand a face-to-face shootout didn't appeal to him either. He glanced about hurriedly, saw his nearest cover in the mist-shrouded trees a little distance up slope to his left. Not hesitating, he yanked the black's head around and used the spur.

The animal bunched its hoofs and lunged strongly up the slope, straight toward the trees. As it did, loose rock turned under its shoes, setting up a noisy clatter—now, at any rate, Little Wolf had had his warning! Not knowing whether the other might be carrying a rifle, Johnny at once flung himself flat along his horse's neck. He thought for an agonizing moment it was going to miss its footing in the rubble and start sliding, but the black dug in and lunged ahead, and then they were in the timber—still without any gunshot following them to break the gloomy morning. Maybe Little Wolf, too, had been caught too much by surprise.

At once, Johnny was off the saddle and turning to hunt his enemy. There was no sign of him.

In that first instant, Johnny Logan could almost have believed the fog had swallowed him again; then he guessed the truth: Little Wolf's reaction, on hearing the noise made by the other rider and perhaps glimpsing him as he vanished into the trees, had been the same as Johnny's—to take cover. The man was there now, up ahead somewhere in this same patch of jack pine, perhaps already prowling in search of him.

His palm turned clammy, grasping the six-gun handle; he had to switch it to the other hand while he dried the sweat against a leg of his jeans. Though both were Indians, Johnny had never had training at a kind of warfare— silently stalking an enemy who at the same time was looking for him—that Little Wolf probably excelled at. Still, it didn't occur to him to retreat: He was not running from Little Wolf, and here in the crowded timber his short gun had an equal chance even against a rifle, if that was what he was up against.

A sound made him whirl, every nerve leaping. There was nothing . . . Then his head lifted and, on a branch slightly above him, he saw a squirrel busily working on a pine cone, turning it over and over in its paws. A fragment tumbled to the ground; he followed its descent with his eye, heard the light tap as it hit and recognized the sound that startled him—one his ears would normally not even have picked up. He shook his head, alarmed at the state of his nerves; he thought, *I've got to get hold of myself!*

Anything was better than waiting here and growing more tense by the minute. Deliberately he started moving forward, picking each step carefully, the six-shooter leveled and ready.

Shifting tree trunks changed their perspective with each slow step he took, gave him new vistas through the crowding stand of skimpy pine. For all his stealth he seemed unable to place a boot without a twig snapping under him. Each time it seemed like a gunshot, that must surely carry directly to the waiting ears of Little Wolf. At last, when his nerves could take no more, he drew close against a fog-damp tree trunk and waited like that for his heartbeat and his breathing to settle.

Tendrils of mist still drifted through the branches, but down here there was no movement, no sound that he could sort out of the constant faint murmur of pine needles, and read as a clue to the approach of his enemy. Patience stretching, he had to down a weird impulse to call out a challenge—do anything, to bring this to an end.

He shifted the weight, was about to step forward again when he froze.

Something seemed vaguely wrong about the outline of a tree, a few yards from him. Johnny stared at it intently, blinking a couple of times when his eyes began to water. Slowly he watched the odd shape change, become a hatbrim; then Little Wolf's face, in profile, seemed to grow from the side of the trunk, under that black felt hat with the eagle feather in its band. Utterly without sound, Little Wolf eased into full view. He crouched, six-shooter thrust out ahead of him—not a rifle, then; he was peering with frightening concentration at something a good distance to Johnny's left.

Johnny Logan swallowed an obstruction in his

throat. His own gun pointed squarely at the man's chest, where the badge was pinned; at this angle and this distance, it would take only a squeeze of the trigger . . .

He couldn't—not even with an enemy as treacherous and dangerous as this renegade Cheyenne, not while his head was turned the other way. Johnny drew a breath. He said quietly, "Little Wolf . . ."

The other seemed to explode into motion, not allowing himself even an instant for the reaction of surprise, or to hunt out the location of the voice. His ears must have told him exactly where Johnny would be standing. Little Wolf was going to ground even as he whirled; and the gun in his fist hammered a shot.

He was too fast.

His bullet missed; he didn't get to try another. Johnny Logan, with shoulders braced against the tree trunk and gun muzzle holding desperately on that rapidly moving form, followed it down and added its sharp report to the echoes of the first one. The hat leaped from Little Wolf's head. He jerked convulsively and then went limp; his head fell. The pistol dropped from his hand into the pine needles, still dribbling smoke.

Johnny was shaking, suddenly, and he had to wait out a long minute before he could break free from where he stood and walk forward, his own gun still gripped tightly. There was really no need of that—the unmoving stillness of the one he had shot told him even before he saw just what his bullet had done to the man's head. He turned convulsively away, barely managed not to be sick. Blindly, he let the revolver off cock and shoved it back into its holster, and stood in the misty chill listening to the small natural sounds around him.

Little Wolf had betrayed his people, had sold out to Sid Walsh for the authority and power of a badge pinned on his chest; he had beaten and tortured Johnny Logan at Walsh's behest, and would have murdered him without a qualm. It didn't matter. To take a life—even such a life as that one—was a sobering business.

There was nothing at all to do for him. With a shake of the head, Johnny turned away, leaving him there, and went back through the trees to where he had tethered the black. In saddle, he remembered the dead man's horse; he went hunting for it, circling wide in order not to have to look again at the body. He found the spotted Indian animal at the timber edge, and took time to untie the reins and loop them over its neck.

Johnny Logan rode on, with the warming sun starting to burn off the last remaining wisps of fog.

Concerning the Bar J, he knew only that it lay somewhere just west of the Reservation. Even in unfamiliar country, though, a range-bred man could make do with directions no more specific than that. A ranch needed water, after all, and grass, and shelter from the fierce Montana storms, and by studying the lay of the land he could limit the possible places to look for these things. Having circled north to avoid the agency headquarters, Johnny Logan felt fairly certain that by bearing south again he should eventually cut a wagon road leading to Jenson's ranch.

Actually, what he found was a well-marked band of hoof tracks, that he interpreted at once as being the drive trail over which Bar J had been in the habit of delivering beef to fill his contract with the agencies. That served as well. He turned the black into it, and less than an hour later a swell of land showed him a spread of log buildings ahead, sod-roofed and mud-chinked, with corrals and holding pastures under fence, and a smear of sunlight bouncing off the whirling blades of a windmill. Johnny gave a grunt of satisfaction, more relieved at his success than he might have admitted. It was not quite midmorning, but he had been hours in the saddle and he was beginning to feel the pressure of narrowing time.

Sometime before noon, Walsh had been told to expect delivery of the McCord cattle. . . .

A couple of men were by the corral, one mounted and waiting for the other to finish putting a saddle on a bay. The first gave Johnny Logan a curious and careful look as he rode up, and then apparently thought he recognized him—Johnny had already remembered the cowpuncher, from the beef ration two days before.

The man's face relaxed into a grin. "Well, by God! It's the bulldoggin' Injun! What are you doing off the Reservation?"

Johnny took the greeting as well-intentioned. He had weighty matters on his own mind and he answered, without preliminary, "I'm looking for Arne Jenson."

"Right yonder." The puncher pointed with his chin, and Johnny saw the rancher coming from the barn, halting while he got a pipe fired up. Johnny thanked the puncher with a nod, and reined over that way.

The cowman shook out his match and squinted a curious eye through the first wreath of pipe smoke, as Johnny Logan dismounted. "Mr. Jenson," the latter said, "I saw you two days ago. In Sid Walsh's office . . ."

"Of course." The man nodded quickly. "You're the young Indian that reamed Walsh out—and tried to back me with that damned Army major." He studied Johnny's face; perhaps he was only now seeing the swellings that still remained there from his beating by the agency police. He said, "As I remember, you don't live on the Reservation. You here looking for a job, maybe?"

"That's not what I had in mind." Johnny hesitated. "I've got some news for you—at least, I think you'll be some concerned when you hear it. Trouble is, I'll have to ask you in advance to take my word for this—I've got no proof."

Interest showed clearly in the other's look. He pursed his lips around the pipestem. "Your word ought to carry some weight with me," he said. "Let's hear what you've got to say."

Johnny laid out for him what he had learned, while Jenson's face grew harder and darker, his mouth drawing down in harsh lines. "So that's it!" the rancher cried finally. "For the first time, McCord's underbidding me begins to make sense! If that bastard has got stuck with beef that should have been destroyed, naturally he'd rather try and dump it, at any price he can get—and however many he might have to split with."

"Of course you understand," Johnny pointed out, "I could be mistaken. . . ."

"You ain't mistaken!" the cowman said grimly. "There's been rumors of cow fever turning up a couple of places, down in McCord's neck of the woods. I guess we know now, they wasn't rumors!" His rope-scarred hand tightened on the bowl of the pipe. "And McCord's got the gall to bring the stuff up here! By God, I been using Bull Flat for hay cuttin', and for winter range—I pay grazing fees to the Cheyenne for the privilege.

Damned if I stand by and let him drive infected stock onto it!"

Suddenly he swung away from Johnny, bawling a command that summoned the two punchers who had been about to ride away from the corral. They came over—the one Johnny had met at the beef ration issue was named, apparently, Dick Stubbs; the other was Bob Early. As they listened their boss threw orders like a general. They were to ride to different sections of the range, pick up any crew members they could find but to be back in no later than an hour, since that was cutting the time as narrow as could safely be risked. Wasting no time with questions, the punchers simply nodded and left on their mission; it looked as though Arne Jenson kept a disciplined crew.

With hoof-stirred saffron dust scattering on a ground wind, the rancher turned again to Johnny; his craggy, weather-beaten face seemed to glow with the challenge of showdown to come. He said, "It's a matter of timing, but with any luck I'll be at the flat waiting when McCord shows with his herd. What happens then is anybody's guess. But I want you to know I appreciate the chance to stop this thing."

Johnny Logan returned his look. "To be perfectly honest with you, my coming here wasn't with an eye to doing you a favor. It's the Cheyenne I'm concerned about; they've had their spirits crushed, and their guns taken away from them so they can't fight their own battles any longer. I thought there was a chance I could get you to help me take on this one."

Narrow-eyed, Jenson studied him a long moment; then he nodded. "You're honest about it, anyway," he said bruskly. "We'll get along . . . and between us we'll give McCord and them others a damn good play for their money!" He added, "You had breakfast?"

"I could use more."

The cowman put a hand on his shoulder, turned him and pointed with his pipestem toward a lean-to tacked onto the end of a long log bunkhouse; smoke rose from the stovepipe chimney, toward the cloud-dotted sky. "Tell Dutch I said to fix you up. And give your horse some grain if he needs it. No need to rush—you got a good half hour at least before we can ride."

"Thanks," Johnny Logan said, and turned to get the black's reins.

CHAPTER XII

Bull Flat was actually a wide meadow, well-grassed and watered, and almost surrounded by lightly timbered hills. Appraising it with a stockman's eye, Johnny could see it as a source of feed and a good, protected winter pasture; he could understand Jenson's anger at the thought of it being deliberately contaminated by a diseased herd.

At the moment it lay empty and ungrazed, and the grass stood high—Jenson probably intending to have a crew in here later, cutting hay. Approaching, now, he led the way over well marked trails and drew rein on a hill spur where there was a view over the flat. The rancher pointed out a southward-opening draw, that probably carried away drainage in wet weather. "There's where McCord will be bringing his beef; it shouldn't be long now. Harry," and he signaled with a waggling thumb to one of his riders, "suppose you scout and see if there's any sign of them."

The puncher named Harry peeled off from the group and rode away down the hill, presently vanishing into the draw. For the moment the rest stayed where they were. There were seven altogether that had ridden from the Bar J—

Jenson had a larger crew than that, but most were scattered over the range on day chores and there hadn't been time to collect more: The sun already stood close to noon.

Dick Stubbs said suddenly, "Rider coming . . ."

He was no more than a dark blot against shining grass, approaching from the flat's north end; but Johnny could have guessed who it was even before Arne Jenson used the glasses he carried on his saddle. The rancher lowered them, his craggy face grim. "Walsh," he said. "Him being here just about confirms what you been telling me, Logan." He put the glasses back into their case.

It occurred to Johnny Logan that Walsh must feel very sure of himself, and of his supremacy over the unhappy Cheyenne, that he would dare to ride alone like this without one of his hand-picked agency police, perhaps, for a bodyguard. Then he thought of another explanation and it turned him slightly cold: Maybe they were all busy hunting *him!* They'd have found Strong Runner, of course, and likely been puzzled by that ugly wound that skewered his throat. By this time, Little Wolf's body could also have been discovered. And Johnny didn't doubt he'd be credited with both killings . . .

Walsh had swung wide to clear the end of this spur, as he approached the mouth of the draw. Jenson spoke to his men and led them unhurriedly down the spur's far slope; when

Walsh came around into view, they were waiting. The agent hauled up sharply, his animal tossing its head uneasily to the sudden pull at the reins. Then Walsh came on, but his narrow face was cautious.

Apparently for the first time, his glance settled on Johnny Logan and the latter could guess at his thoughts. Jenson didn't leave him long with them. "So," he said coldly. "Got a little deal going in beef, have you, Sid?"

"A deal?" Walsh looked at the rancher. He plainly decided he could get away with a bluff. "What are you talking about? It was explained to you—I don't make deals anymore. That's been taken out of my hands."

"I heard the explanation," Arne Jenson said, his look and his tone unyielding. "But I heard this was a deal with some angles to it. Angles I thought I better look into!"

Suddenly Walsh lost his aplomb. He looked at Johnny and he almost shouted: "You going to believe what some damned Indian tells you? You going to take his word against a white man?"

The drum of hoofs interrupted Jenson's reply. It was the puncher, Harry, returning. He was using the spur, and he shouted his news before he reached them: "Cattle coming, boss! A big bunch of 'em—and they sure as hell don't look good!"

Jenson thanked him with a nod. Still not answering Sid Walsh's outburst, he gave a look to Dick Stubbs; the latter quickly kneed his mount toward Walsh's as the agent, taking alarm, started to back away. He stopped when he saw the muzzle of the gun the cowboy aimed at him. Reaching an arm, Stubbs flipped open the front of Walsh's coat and revealed the weapon shoved behind his waistband. He deftly captured it.

Sid Walsh started an angry protest. "Shut up!" Jenson told him, in such a tone that he subsided. "I'm making you responsible for him," the rancher told Stubbs, who nodded. After that Jenson wheeled his horse and led off toward the draw at a good clip; and Dick Stubbs snatched the reins from the prisoner's hands and towed him along, keeping him always aware of the threat of that drawn gun.

The draw descended rather steeply, scattered with rubble that had washed down from higher up. Johnny Logan, at Jenson's stirrup, grew aware of familiar sound somewhere ahead— the melancholy sound of cattle on the move and protesting it, the bawling in many throats echoing off the steep rock walls. Presently a shift in the course of the draw brought them to a turn, and rounding this they suddenly reined in as they saw the forefront of the herd crowding the narrow passage, with riders visible through streaking dust and bars of sunlight, yelling and pushing the cattle hard.

Arne Jenson swore.

The leaders were apt to be the strongest and toughest animals in a drive—and anyone could see even the leaders of this one were in a bad way. Johnny Logan stared aghast, seeing the shambling gait, the drooping heads, the ropy saliva that dripped from their jaws into the dust. He wondered that they were on their feet at all, or that they could have been driven any distance. He would bet that not all of them had made it.

He could imagine the herders pushing them mercilessly, stopping for nothing, letting the dead and dying lie where they happened to fall. From the way the survivors came on, almost at a stumbling run, the herders must be in a hurry now with the end of the trail in sight, to get the last of them off their hands—to be rid of what was left and get the distressful sound of bawling, suffering cattle out of their ears, the stench of sickness out of their nostrils.

He thought he had never seen anyone so angry as Arne Jenson. The rancher had the rifle from his saddle boot; standing in the stirrups, he brandished the weapon as he turned to shout at his crew: "Stop them! Keep them off the flat! I don't want a single head getting past us onto that grass!" And then the rifle was at his shoulder and he was firing, as fast as he could work the ejector, into the mass of cattle crowding through the draw.

As his crew followed orders, the racket of

gunfire swelled deafeningly and cattle began to go down. They were packed together closely enough that it was impossible to miss—and for most of them, Johnny Logan thought, it could only be a merciful death. Lacking a saddle gun, he had drawn his revolver, but he held off using it—something told him he had better hang onto the five bullets it contained. Ears ringing to heavy gunfire echoing between the narrow walls, he stayed close to Jenson's stirrup and kept pace as the latter rode ahead into the stench of smoke and spilled blood.

He kept expecting they would run into an answering fire, but so far there had been none. He'd heard some shouting, mingled with the rising bellow of frightened cattle; the herders, that could be glimpsed briefly through smoke and dust, seemed to be having their hands full with the herd. The terrified animals were fighting now to make an about-face, despite the press of their numbers—to turn their backs and retreat back down the draw, out of this nightmare of noise and muzzle flash and the smell of death.

Once Johnny thought he heard Jenson say, above the hubbub: "There's McCord!" At the same moment he had a glimpse, above the lunging backs and glinting horns, of a man who appeared briefly in the drift of smoke and dust. Johnny Logan saw his face . . . and recognized him!

To his surprise, he knew he had seen the man once before—under the tall pine tree at Spellman's trading post, three days ago, standing beside his horse and absorbed in talk with Sergeant Bailey. Johnny had completely forgotten the incident; but apparently Bailey hadn't, and it answered a question that had been nagging at Johnny all along. Although he actually hadn't overheard a word the two were saying, when he came up on them that day, it began to look as though Ed Bailey was convinced he had. The conviction must have been strong enough to lead to the order being given for Johnny to be picked up, and kept from warning Major Harriman in any way about the conspiracy afoot between the sergeant and McCord.

It had all been a mistake on Bailey's part, of course—and it had ruined what could have been a simple operation. Except for that mistake, and its consequences, Johnny Logan's suspicions would never have been roused; the conspiracy need not have come to light.

The irony of it struck him hard and he would have liked to tell somebody, only there was no one to tell just now in this confusion of gun-sound, of shouting men and bawling cattle and frightened squeals of horses.

Somewhere ahead a gun flashed, and at the ripping sound a bullet made passing him within inches, Johnny involuntarily check reined the black. But that was the only shot anyone fired at him. A swirl of dust, sent up by the hoofs of scrambling steers, shook like a curtain above their backs and Johnny's brief look at Nels McCord and the other riders was snatched away. They all, he thought, likely had all they could do to manage their horses, and keep from being impaled on the wildly tossing horns as the herd turned on them in panic.

Arne Jenson meanwhile was pressing them hard, yelling his men on; it meant picking a way among the bodies of downed steers, some of them already stiffening in death and others still kicking feebly. Nor had they all been killed by bullets—Johnny was certain that a good many, already enfeebled by disease and practically dying on their feet, must have gone down under the horns and trampling hoofs of the stronger.

And then abruptly the lower end of the draw emptied out onto a wide rocky slope, that lay against a bare fault rim of sheer granite rising a couple of hundred feet on the north and east. Here, as they broke into the open, Jenson's riders were met without warning by a barrage of rifle fire.

It was a wild moment. Johnny Logan found himself fighting to control the black, while he glanced ahead and saw that McCord's men had room at last to shake loose of the frenzied cattle, and were turning to give battle. A Bar J hand doubled over, nearly fell against Johnny Logan as he fell sideways from the saddle. Johnny managed to avoid him—and then, just at his stirrup, Arne Jenson's animal gave an odd sound like a cough as lead struck it. Johnny turned in time to see the rifle spin out of the cowman's hands when the horse under him plowed headlong into the ground. Jenson tried to leap clear. He almost made it, but when he landed one boot was caught under his animal's weight.

Johnny Logan was aware of this. He fired at a McCord rider, knew he missed; next moment he was sawing at the rein in an effort to keep his own horse from colliding with the other and piling up. There was no need for thought. Hurriedly he leaped down, still holding the reins, while he saw how it was with Jenson.

He caught the desperate look the man threw him. The leg was trapped, beyond the rancher's ability to pull free. Johnny gave him a shout of encouragement and bent to help, but quickly found he had to let go of the reins and use both hands in order to get sufficient grip. As he did so a bullet struck a rock beside him, sprayed chips against his boot. He gritted his teeth and threw his weight into the work. A grunt of pain broke from Jenson; at the same moment he pulled free. And Johnny looked up in time to see the black—stung, perhaps, by a glancing bullet—go racing back into the shelter of the draw through a confusion of Bar J riders, its reins and stirrups flopping.

Arne Jenson was trying to get to his feet but he fell back when the numbed leg gave way. Seeing that, Johnny Logan knew that reaching the draw would be out of the question. So would leaving him here, helpless. He looked hastily around for the nearest possible shelter, then stooped and hooked the man's arm over his shoulder. "This way," he grunted, and began to half lead and half drag him.

It was not much when they got there—a shallow erosion gully, no more than a wrinkle in the barren earth. Up close it looked even shallower, but Johnny shoved the other man in and followed at a flat dive. He narrowly beat out a bullet that showered him with a stinging cloud of grit. Panting as he hugged the narrow trench, he pawed his eyes clear and heard still more bullets strike and whine away in rebound.

Presently all gunfire petered out. In the gully where he crouched there was stillness. At his elbow, he heard Arne Jenson ask tightly, "You hurt?"

He hadn't done the bandaged rib any good, but he ignored it. "No. You?"

"Just this damned hoof I twisted when my bronc fell . . . Kid, I got to thank you for pulling me clear."

Johnny grunted something. He had his breathing

194

under control; he pushed hair back from his sweating, dust-layered face and, gripping his revolver, raised himself to try for a look at what was happening.

Of Arne Jenson's crew he could see nothing at all, so they must have retreated into the draw; he could only guess whether they had stopped there to regroup, or kept on going. Out on the open rocky slope, where sunlight bouncing off the steep granite cliff was a bright dazzle, the scattered herd was being regathered. Johnny Logan estimated its size at something under four hundred head, and McCord seemed to have brought more than enough men to handle them.

He saw all this in a single sweeping glance, that also took in an eye-stabbing smear of sunlight on the barrel of Jenson's rifle, lying in the dirt a half dozen yards away; it might as well have been a half mile. For, no sooner had he shown himself than another rifle shot flatted off, the bullet striking close enough to make him pull back again . . . but not before he had glimpsed the one who fired it, and the blue shirt and yellow chevrons that identified the rider as Sergeant Bailey.

A clump of bushes grew at the edge of the gully, a little farther along; Johnny Logan went scrambling for it on elbows and knees and, using it as a screen, raised himself this time more cautiously. He found that in order to see he had to move one of the lower branches slightly with his pistol barrel. His nerves were taut, in full expectation that one of his enemies would see the movement and fire at it.

Instead, there was a sudden drum of hoofbeats and he was just in time to see a rider burst out of the mouth of the draw. His first thought was that it might be one of the Bar J crewmen, making some insane kind of charge; then he saw that the rider was Sid Walsh, who apparently had either been turned loose or, in the confusion, somehow managed to escape from those who were holding him. Johnny brought up his gun, but wind rattling the brush hampered him and before he could get a shot the man was out of range, spurring hard. Johnny swore angrily.

Arne Jenson crawled up, dragging his injured leg. "What happened?"

"Nothing much. Except we just lost our hostage—for whatever he might have been worth to us."

"Walsh?"

Johnny Logan pointed with his gun-barrel. They could see McCord and Sergeant Bailey riding out to meet the Indian agent; they came together to exchange serious talk, while the wind whipped dust at them and the work of regathering the scattered herd went forward.

Johnny said, "I'm wondering how Walsh was able to get away. I saw one of your men take a bad hit—I don't know which one; but that should have left four of them to hold the draw, and hang onto the prisoner."

"Maybe," Jenson said gruffly. "And maybe not! Those are fair, run-of-the-mine cowhands, but they ain't what you'd call fightin' men— they wasn't hired for that. If they saw my horse go down, they may be figuring me for dead. In which case, it would hardly be surprising if they just turned Sid Walsh loose and took off, rather than fight a pointless battle. Seems like *I* would, under like circumstances."

Scowling, Johnny Logan studied the entrance to the draw, unable to get any hint at the situation there. He said, "Well, we may get the answer fairly quick. I have an idea McCord is about to make a second try—only this time, it looks like he means to use his herd for a battering ram, and run right over any opposition."

"Don't count on him finding any . . ."

Once again Johnny Logan eyed that rifle lying out there in the sun, a shimmer of polished metal. If he could only get his hands on it, the story might be different; but he didn't think he had any chance at all. He thought his enemies must be well aware of it there. It would be just like Ed Bailey to leave it for bait, trying to tempt Johnny into the open where he could be knocked off.

At the moment, the only movement near the gully was the big, green-bodied fly that had appeared from somewhere, drawn by the smell of blood, to explore the stiffening carcass of Jenson's dead horse. It circled in the sun, gleaming iridescently. The heat collecting about them, and the buzzing dance of the fly, held something almost hypnotic.

Johnny turned attention to the revolver in his hand. He punched out the spent shell, replacing it from his belt loops, and while he was at it slipped an extra into the chamber he normally carried empty, for the hammer to rest on. The weapon had been little use to him so far in this situation; still, before that herd could enter the draw it would have to come within short-gun range. When it did he meant to do what damage as he could— drop as many of the infected steers as he was able and, with luck, perhaps even break up the forward thrust of the drive. Beside him, he heard the gun-hammer go back full cock and knew that Jenson had the same thought. It was a lot for two men, armed only with pistols, to accomplish . . . especially when, the moment they opened fire, they could count on being targets themselves. . . .

"They're rolling!" Arne Jenson said tersely.

Suddenly, on a signal, McCord's men were in motion—yelling and spurring their horses as they fired off guns, or flapped coiled ropes at the flanks of the cattle to start them. Their shouts echoed thinly off the granite cliff, swelled by the bawls of exhausted and probably dying steers. They were pointing straight at the mouth of the draw, and the ground shook to the rumble of hoofs and dust began rising in a yellow stain toward the deep sky.

Revolver solid in his hand, Johnny Logan controlled his breathing while he waited for the moment to open fire. Then, while the point of the herd was still some hundred yards out of range, something drew his eye upward to the rim of the cliff.

He squinted against the dazzle of sun-bright rock and made out the figure standing sharply etched there, against blue sky and billowing white cloud . . . a man who stood half-naked, black hair blowing in the wind, streaks of paint and the bow in his hands clearly visible. It was like looking at a figure out of myth—or out of a time now vanished, when sight of an Indian in war paint and battle dress could make an enemy's blood run cold.

Now, even as Johnny Logan stared, the man on the cliff-top flexed his bow, and loosed his arrow.

It made a silver streak in the sun. Down below, a rider in cavalry blue had reined in to watch the herd move past—it was Burkhart, who had acted last night as Sergeant Bailey's messenger. Johnny Logan saw the trooper's whole body jerk as the arrow, arcing true, struck home. His campaign hat fell to the ground; his arms flung wide and he toppled slowly after it, the feathered shaft like an ugly growth between his shoulder blades.

The killing, silent as it was, might have gone unnoticed if one of McCord's punchers hadn't happened to glance that way, at just that moment. Johnny saw him stiffen, and twist in the saddle for a look upward at the man on the rim. Next moment he was wigwagging frantically with the saddle gun he carried; his cry of warning barely sounded above the commotion of moving cattle. He pulled his horse to a halt, and put the rifle to his shoulder and threw off a hurried shot.

It missed, but it caught attention. Others turned to see what was happening; even as they did, the Indian was no longer alone. Johnny Logan counted at least eight more of them suddenly lining the rim, kneeling or standing as they sent arrows raining down the slant of air. One even had a single-shot rifle that he must have kept carefully hidden away from the white conquerors—he was firing as fast as he could shove cartridges into the breech, though he couldn't keep up with the bow-handlers' accuracy or speed.

The distance was extreme for Indian arrows, but with the drive so closely bunched they could hardly fail to find some kind of target. Cattle began to go down; one cowpuncher took a spinning tumble when his horse fell, as though it had been chopped from under him. What had been a herd became all at once a confused milling in streaking dust, and a racket of yelling men and bawling animals and answering rifle fire. Johnny Logan saw one Indian struck by a bullet and spun about, to drop from sight.

And then Johnny had recovered from his first surprise and was on his feet, scrambling up the crumbling bank of the gully. No one paid him any attention at all as he made for Jenson's rifle. He snatched it up, shook the dust from its barrel, jacked a shell into the chamber—and went motionless, the weapon utterly forgotten.

The horseman had appeared while he wasn't looking. He was poised up there at the very edge of the cliff, lance held aloft—unmoving, as though he defied his enemies to target him. The horse, like the man, was daubed with painted symbols; eagle feather fluttered, braided into its mane. Johnny thought he would have known the rider, even if he hadn't recognized the animal as Swooping Hawk's paint pony.

So this was Swooping Hawk's answer to his plea for help, against those who would bring disease and death to the Reservation. These were the ones Leads-His-Horse had told about—misguided young men of the Cheyenne, who had chosen his son as their leader, and who spent their days in idle war-play and dreams of glory that were past. Foolish, undisciplined, and unthinking, they must see this as their chance at last to strike a blow in revenge against the white-eyes. . . .

It occurred to Johnny that Swooping Hawk was searching for something, now, in that confusion below him of dust and milling cattle, of squealing horses and shouting men and bellowing rifles. All at once he seemed to find it. The young fellow's head lifted sharply, the lance dropped into position—clamped beneath his arm, the point leveled and ready to strike.

And then man and horse took off from the cliff's edge.

Johnny Logan sucked in his breath, horrified— certain that the animal had lost its footing, to drop them both those two hundred feet to certain death. But, no! Before his astonished eyes, they were both plummeting straight down—the man seated erect with hair blown back, one arm flung high and the other holding the lance braced beneath his elbow; the pony, with hoofs bunched and mane and tail streaming in the wind of their descent. And Johnny felt the eyes starting from his head.

Surely it was some simple trick of perspective, he told himself, or of the brilliant light—the granite cliff couldn't possibly be as steep as it looked from here. Swooping Hawk must have known his surefooted pony could make the slide in safety. Yet something cold seemed to touch him and raise the hairs at the back of his neck, as he remembered the young brave's boastful tale of his vision of Heammawihio—the Wise One

202

Above—and of the great warrior bird that had been sent him, in a trance, to teach him the secret of its unerring descent to strike its prey, with the hawk's invincible swiftness and strength. . . .

Swooping Hawk had reached the foot of the cliff. For just an instant the pony seemed about to stumble. Then it caught its footing and plunged forward; and in that moment, through drifting dust and the scattered movement of frightened steers, Johnny saw the brave's intended quarry.

Agent Walsh—the arch-enemy, the oppressor of the People—was afoot, at the moment; apparently an arrow, striking his horse in the muscle of one foreleg, had lamed it and he had stepped down to examine the damage. Now, however, he straightened—and saw Swooping Hawk bearing toward him, leaning forward with the lance leveled. Helplessly Walsh started backing away, a futile effort to escape. For in the next instant Swooping Hawk was upon him, and a savage sweep of his arm drove the point of the ashwood lance straight at the man's chest.

As it struck, Walsh seemed to shrivel—like a spider that has been stepped on. Convulsively he clutched the shaft of the lance with both hands and, hugging it to him like that, was hurled violently to the ground. Swooping Hawk left the spear in his body, reining his pony aside just in time to avoid trampling him; his head flung back, a cry of pure triumph sounded from the young brave's throat.

Everything else had seemed to stand still, during Swooping Hawk's incredible plunge down the sheer cliff face. Now, belatedly, men broke from their momentary paralysis. Out of the corner of his eye Johnny Logan saw Sergeant Bailey sighting a rifle; it reminded him that he held one in his own hands. In desperate haste he turned, flinging it up, but Bailey was ahead of him. Smoke and spurting flame leaped from the sergeant's weapon, above the lunging shapes of terror-stricken cattle; and to the slap of the report, Swooping Hawk was wiped cleanly off his paint pony's back.

Johnny Logan managed then to get off his own shot, and saw Bailey sag and drop his rifle, and grab the saddle to keep from falling. Numbly, he lowered his smoking weapon, as Arne Jenson hobbled up from the gully to join him, and riders—some of them in U. S. Cavalry blue—came pouring out of the draw.

It was all too late . . . just as his own reactions had been too slow to allow him to save Swooping Hawk. . . .

CHAPTER XIII

Nels McCord, at short range, turned out to be a hard-eyed, tight-lipped man who fell back on cold bluff as he stood facing Major Harriman in the agency headquarters. "You can't prove anything against me," he said crisply. "Since that herd was never actually delivered, you've got no case."

"I think we can put one together," the major told him bluntly. "I've already had a word with that clerk of Walsh's—he knows a considerable amount about his boss's dealings and is all too happy to talk. And with what we got from Sergeant Bailey before he died, I'm pretty certain we'll have you on a charge of conspiring to defraud the U. S. Government." He jerked his head toward the door. "Now, get out!"

McCord looked at him blackly. He turned to Johnny Logan, standing with arms folded and shoulders leaning tiredly against the door frame. Their stares locked; then, with an angry shrug, McCord turned and stalked past him, out of the building.

Slanting light of afternoon, streaking through the windows, filled the room with a golden dance of dust motes. The major, pacing restlessly, passed a hand down over his fleshy features and turned to include Johnny and Arne Jenson in his glance. "Before I leave here—which won't be for a day or two—I'm going to want full statements from both of you, as to just what happened here today; also, anything else you can tell me that might be of help. All right?"

The rancher nodded. Johnny Logan had a question. "Major, what became of the two Indians who were killed?"

"I turned them over to their friends; the bodies should be on the way home by now." Johnny thought of Leads-His-Horse, and of the grief there would be tonight in the lodge of Swooping Hawk's father. Harriman must have read his look, for the major nodded and said harshly, "This has been a sad business. It could have been much worse, except for your part in stopping it. They could have got away with their scheme—slaughtered the beef and destroyed the evidence—and no telling how many of the Cheyenne might have died from eating tainted beef. I shudder to think of it, because it would have been my mistake." He looked at Jenson. "I know now, too, I should have listened when you warned me McCord couldn't underbid you, unless he was involved in something underhanded. It goes without saying, the contract is yours again until further notice."

"Whatever you say," the rancher answered gruffly—still a little angry with the major, Johnny Logan thought.

Harriman went on: "I predict there's going to be a great deal more experimenting, before the problem of supply for the reservation is solved. No telling how many ideas the Army and the Indian Bureau, too, will be coming up with. Meanwhile, I've asked Howard Cummings if he'll take over and hold down this office, until there's been time to appoint a successor for Walsh. I'm recommending that he be considered for the post, but of course the Bureau will do what they please."

"He's an honest man," Johnny said, "and a good friend to the Indian." He came close to adding, *Which may be against him!* But that was no more than weary cynicism. It had been a long day, and a hard one; he had seen death, and greed, and blind, foolhardy courage. He had seen much that he was yet to absorb.

A moment later, leaving the office, he was stopped by Arne Jenson as the latter caught up with him outside the door. The rancher laid a hand on his shoulder. "I ain't a man who finds it easy to say thanks," Jenson told him, without preliminary, "but I owe you a few—aside from saving my life for me. Anyway, if you happen to want a job, there's one for you at the Bar J. Any time."

Johnny thought about that. "I got no plans," he said. "But I just might be taking you up on that."

"Any time," Jenson said again, and walked off

to where his crew and their horses were waiting for him to join them and leave for home, their work here finished. It had been a long day for them, too. Johnny watched them ride away.

There was considerable activity around the agency buildings. The squad of troopers who had ridden with Major Harriman from Fort Dilson were at work making camp—tents going up, cookfires starting, horses being led out to water and feed thrown down for them. Shadows and slanting shafts of sunlight were both growing long across the dust. Johnny's black stood waiting at the hitch rail, none the worse for its part in the day's action.

Someone called his name. He turned quickly, and saw Anne standing beside her pony. He went to her, and she caught both his hands while those big, dark eyes of hers anxiously studied his face. "You're all right?" she exclaimed. "I've been hearing terrible rumors about what happened."

"It was bad enough," he said. "You heard about Swooping Hawk?" And at her solemn nod: "I saw what he did—and it's still more than I can believe. Anyway, I'll try to tell you the whole thing."

"First," she said, interrupting, "I know how tired you must be—but do you think you'd be able to do a little more riding?"

"Today? I suppose that would depend."

"It's Lame Elk," the girl explained. "Owl

Woman sent me word—she's shown him the pouch, and he wants to talk to you."

Weary as he was, Johnny Logan felt the quick stirring of excitement. "Then I'd better go! You'll come with me? Wait till I get my horse, and we can do our talking while we ride. . . ."

Dusk was settling as they entered the Cheyenne village, the lazy sounds of evening rising from the flat where the tepees bunched their poles against the paling sky; sparks from cookfires streaked away on the wind that carried the aromas of woodsmoke and broiling meat. As they had yesterday, Johnny and the girl picked their way among the lodges, with the life of the village about them and kids and dogs underfoot. At one point Johnny suddenly pulled rein, looking at a man who stood alone before his lodge, wrapped in a blanket and in a silence of grief. "Leads-His-Horse," he murmured. "I ought to say something to him. . . ."

Anne reached a restraining hand to touch his own. "Not just now. He mourns his son. It would be wrong to intrude."

"All right," Johnny said, and they rode on in silence to Lame Elk's lodge.

Here, as before, Owl Woman met them and without a word invited them to enter the tepee. Lame Elk might not have moved at all since yesterday, from his backrest near the firepit; but now he lifted his head and Johnny saw what had not been there the last time—a glint of intelligence, in the dark eyes that looked at him from the incredibly wrinkled face. At Owl Woman's gesture Johnny seated himself, cross-legged, facing the old man who so far had neither spoken, nor made any gesture with the arthritic hands that lay crumpled in his lap. Anne, as though knowing her place, had withdrawn into the shadows.

Johnny waited. Now Owl Woman brought a long-stemmed pipe which she gave her husband, and held a glowing brand from the fire for him; he puffed the pipe alight, sucking noisily and deeply while his sunken cheeks hollowed themselves alarmingly over toothless gums. Apparently this was to be a matter of ritual and formality. As Johnny watched, Lame Elk blew puffs of smoke in offering to the earth, to the sky above the circular smoke-hole, to each cardinal point of the compass, the gray and straggling hair brushing the shoulders of his buckskins. He offered the pipe to Johnny, who carefully copied his moves and then handed it back into the bony claw. Owl Woman stepped forward to take the pipe, and retreated again.

Lame Elk spoke, in a wheezing and broken remnant of what must once have been a powerful voice. A few words only; then he lapsed into silence, plainly expecting an answer. Johnny looked over at Anne and heard her interpret:

"Lame Elk says he would have known, anywhere, the son of Striking Bear."

Striking Bear. . . .

So he knew at last the name of his father, and the meaning of the painting on the medicine bag. A breath filled Johnny's chest, a swelling sensation of a quest fulfilled. He said carefully, "Tell Lame Elk, I've traveled a good many suns trying to learn something about my father and my people. Tell him I'll sure appreciate hearing anything at all he might remember."

This in turn was translated into the old man's tongue. He did not seem to hear, and for a moment Johnny Logan feared he had retreated again into vacant senility. But then he began to talk, and Johnny listened—not understanding a word, but fascinated by the liquid sound of the language itself pouring into the stillness of the lodge, and the accompanying eloquent gestures of those crippled hands. For Lame Elk seemed to gather vitality and strength as he spoke, bringing the distant past once more to life.

Anne's quiet voice took over. "Johnny, he says no one is likely to have remembered your father because Striking Bear was of the Southern Cheyenne. We're all one people, as you know; and in those days, before the white man's reservations finally split us in two, there was much traveling of long distances and visiting back and forth between us. One summer, Striking

211

Bear brought several lodges up to Montana from the southern ranges. He met Lame Elk, and they became good friends. He was still a young man; but Lame Elk says that, even then, he had the promise of becoming a mighty leader. And as a token of their friendship, Lame Elk offered to paint the magic symbols of power on the sacred medicine bag of your father, that you now own.

"But then the white man's sickness came upon the People—cholera, he means. Lame Elk was stricken and lay as one dead; in fact, he says he was picked up and carried to the home of the spirits, in the sky. He finally returned to his body and lived again, but weeks had passed. Many had died. And Striking Bear and his followers had vanished—gone south, Lame Elk supposed. He never saw or heard of them again, until today when Owl Woman showed him your father's pouch . . . and when you entered the lodge, and he saw Striking Bear's face in yours. . . ."

For a long moment Johnny could not speak. "It adds up," he said finally. "I understood it was the cholera he was fleeing, when he went out to the Bitterroots . . . to be massacred, just as though he and the rest had been wiped off the face of the earth!"

There was more talk, after that. Lame Elk wanted to hear about Johnny's years as a member of a white rancher's household, and he kept his aged, red-rimmed eyes pinned on his visitor's face as Anne repeated the latter's words in the Cheyenne tongue. Owl Woman brought wooden bowls of food and they ate as they talked—until Johnny happened to glance at the old Indian and saw his crumpled hands lying idle in his lap, his head sunk forward on his breast. Lame Elk was asleep.

Johnny hurried to take his departure, apologetic at having worn the old man out without meaning to. As he was about to duck through the opening of the lodge, Owl Woman stopped him, holding out to him the medicine bag he had left with her. He saw that she had done some work on it: The broken ends of thong had been replaced now with new rawhide, so that it could once more be worn about the neck of its owner. Johnny slipped the thong over his head, and thanked her with a smile and a touch of his hand on her shoulder.

Anne was waiting when he stepped out into the early darkness. She said softly, "Well—John Striking Bear . . . Have you learned what you wanted? Or do you want to look further, among the Southern Cheyenne?"

He hesitated. "I don't really know. That would mean a long trip—to the Indian Nations, almost as far as Texas and no reason to think I'd learn any more than Lame Elk could tell me. For now, I reckon I'm satisfied." They stood together, under the first stars, with the canvas of the tepees glowing from their inner fires. Voices of the village came to them; a nighthawk swooped above their heads, on silent wings.

Johnny said softly, "Do you know, in spite of all the Cheyenne have suffered—there's peace here."

Beside him, the girl asked, "Are you telling me you've decided you want to stay?"

Something in her tone made him try to see her face, but he couldn't in the thickening dusk. He said, "You don't want me to stay . . ."

"For your sake, Johnny—no. I can't help feeling it would be a bad mistake. To go to the blanket? To be a reservation Indian—with nothing better to look forward to, in our lifetime at least, except live on the white man's charity? It was a dead end for Swooping Hawk. For you, I'm afraid it could be even worse."

For a long moment he didn't answer. At last he said, "I'm afraid you might be right. I'm always going to be left somewhere in the middle, I guess. Yesterday, part of me was plain jealous when I heard Swooping Hawk tell about his vision . . . the same part that wants to believe I really saw what I thought I did this afternoon, that he actually dived unhurt off that cliff, like a bird of prey falling on its enemy. But in my heart, I know it must have been that my eyes fooled me. Just as I know it's useless, raised the way I was, to think I could ever have a vision . . . or actually believe in Heammawihio!"

214

Anne slipped her warm hand into his—a sign that she had understood. He squeezed her fingers, and drew a long breath. "No, Anne. I have to go on. Where, I don't know yet. Arne Jenson has offered me a riding job; maybe I'll take him up on it, for the time being. It will give me a chance to be near you, and to see how things work out with the new agent, whoever he turns out to be.

"But, I don't know if I'm going to be satisfied spending all my life as a cowhand, either. Maybe it's simply hopeless—maybe I'll never find my place in the white man's world. Or if I'm lucky, maybe someday I will—and while I'm at it, a way too to do something for my people." He shook his head a little, at the size of the quest that lay before him. "Well, all I know for sure is, I'll never find what I want unless I start looking!"

"You'll find it, Johnny," she said quietly, as they listened to the sounds of the summer night. "However long it takes, I know you will. And remember—however long it takes—I'll always be wanting to know how it is with you.

"Please don't ride away and forget me, Johnny Logan!"

She meant it. She sounded almost frightened. Johnny slipped his arm about her waist.

"Forget you, Anne?" he said, and he meant it too. "That just ain't very likely. . . ."

Center Point Large Print
600 Brooks Road / PO Box 1
Thorndike, ME 04986-0001 USA

(207) 568-3717

US & Canada:
1 800 929-9108
www.centerpointlargeprint.com